SCARS THAT SHINE

A Hustler's Tale

SCARS THAT SHINE

A Hustler's Tale

A Novel by

Santosh Verma

BLACKSPINE®
WISDOM THROUGH KNOWLEDGE
VELVET ARC
An imprint of
Blackspine Publishing Pvt. Ltd.

BLACKSPINE PUBLISHING PVT LTD
Head Office: C-29, Sector 7, Noida, UP, NCR, 201301
Phone: +91 98102-28588,+91-120-3685804,3131027
E-mail: info@blackspinepublishing.com
Website: www.blackspinepublishing.com

First published by Velvet Arc,
an imprint of Blackspine Publishing Pvt. Ltd.

First Edition 2026
ISBN 978-93-49453-08-1

Printed in India

Dedicated

to

All who transform
scars into fuel for growth
Their courage makes them shine

Acknowledgement

First and foremost, I bow in gratitude to my parents, who brought me into this world and laid the foundation of who I am today. Their blessings and values continue to guide me on my journey.

I also acknowledge the situations and challenges that tested me, broke me at times, yet made me strong enough to rise and shine again. Without those struggles, this book would not have been possible.

My deepest thanks to all my school and college friends, and to my female acquaintances, for their presence and support in shaping my path.

To my brother, Sudesh Verma, who helped me move from Ranchi to Delhi, I remain grateful for your strength and encouragement.

To my sister, Vinnie, who inspired me to share my experiences in writing, this book carries your spirit in every page.

To my wife, Juhi, who lovingly tolerated my mood swings and stood resiliently beside me, thank you for transforming my challenges into strength and partnership.

Aryan and Ankush, my beloved nephews, you are my pride and my endless joy. Khushboo and Raunak, who forever see me as a superstar—you remind me of the light within. And Isha and Setu, for being part of this journey.

To my daughter, Muskaan, my lifeline—your love and encouragement inspired me to step outside the routine and ordinary, to create something that reflects hope and courage. This book belongs to you as much as it does to me.

I also extend my heartfelt thanks to my brother-in-law, Major General Sinha, for his unwavering support and inspiring presence. To my brother, Dr. Sarvesh Verma, whose encouragement and wisdom continue to strengthen me, I owe deep gratitude. To my sister-in-law (Bhabhi), whom I have known since before her marriage and who became part of our family through her bond with Sudesh Verma, I thank you warmly for your affection and support. And to my eldest sister-in-law, Anju Verma, your kindness and presence have added so much light to my journey—I remain truly grateful.

Finally, I offer my heartfelt thanks to all the pure souls who touched my life and lifted me beyond boundaries. Your kindness and faith have helped me rise, and for that, I will always be grateful.

—Santosh Verma

Contents

Preface

When I look back on my journey, it feels less like a story and more like a pilgrimage. A boy from Ranchi, once dismissed for his failures, set out not just to earn a living, but to seek meaning. Along the way, I was tested—by betrayal, by silence, by loss that tore through me like fire.

The death of my nephew Ankush was my deepest wound. His laughter still echoes in my ears, sometimes in the quiet of the night, sometimes in the middle of a crowded room. A sound so pure, so innocent, now forever out of reach. His absence hollowed me, shattered me, and yet, strangely, it also remade me. In grief, I discovered both the fragility of life and the unbreakable strength of love. It was as if God had placed me before a mirror and asked: *"Will you let this break you, or will you rise carrying his light within you?"*

The company I built was never only about books.

Every page printed, every word a child read, was a silent prayer—an offering to Ankush. It was my way of whispering to him: *"Your spirit lives here. You did not vanish—you became the ink, the story, the knowledge that guides others forward."*

But my story is not only of loss. Through storms of betrayal and nights of crushing loneliness, I found unexpected anchors. My daughter, Misha, became my compass. Her innocent words steadied me whenever I faltered: *"Papa, you are my hero."* In her eyes, I discovered the truest definition of success—not wealth, not applause, not recognition, but presence. To be there when she needed me. To rise even when broken. To love without fear.

Yet life tested me in ways I never imagined. I faced betrayals not just from strangers but from those I once trusted as family. Relatives who measured compassion in equity stakes. Mentors who turned into rivals. A pandemic that stripped away every certainty. At times, I sold everything I had, down to my car and my wife's jewellery, not because I was weak, but because I refused to let my employees—the family I built—suffer alone.

This book is part fiction, part autobiography—woven through the life of Samarth. And when you turn these pages, know this: my story is not of a perfect man. It is of a flawed, often broken human being who stumbled, bled, and yet chose, again and again, to rise. My scars became my scriptures. My losses became my teachers. My resilience became my prayer.

If even one reader finds courage here—to endure betrayal without losing hope, to survive a loss without losing love, to rise after falling again and again—then my story will have fulfilled its purpose.

Because the truth is simple: life will wound you. People will test you. Fate will strip you bare. But love, if held with faith, will always resurrect you.

With love,
—Santosh Verma

Foreword

There are books you read and forget. And then there are books that stay with you long after the last page is turned—because they are not crafted from imagination, but from lived truths, raw and unflinching. Scars That Shine belongs to the latter.

When I first approached this manuscript, I thought I knew the man who wrote it. In the years I have known him, he has always struck me as calm, composed, generous—a man whose kindness seemed effortless, whose optimism appeared unshakable. He carried himself lightly, rarely revealing the weight within. But as I read, I realised how little I had known of his scars, how much of his journey he had kept hidden behind silence.

I did not know of the betrayals—by a brother he once trusted, by a cousin who toyed with his desperation, by a mentor who sought to block his rise. I did not know of the nights he sat alone under the buzz of a dying tube light, staring at ledgers that betrayed him more cruelly than words. I did not know of the pandemic days when he sold his beloved XUV, pawned his wife's jewellery, and still stood firm so his employees would not be abandoned. I did not know the full depth of his grief when Ankush, whose laughter once filled his world, was snatched away by fate.

Reading these pages, I often paused with tears in my eyes. And I confess: again and again, one thought pierced me—*I wish I had known. I wish I had known his pain earlier, so that I could have stood beside him, even if only in silence. So that he would not have carried it alone.*

But perhaps that is who he is. A man who bore his burdens quietly, never making his scars the burden of others. A man who turned anguish into empathy, betrayal into wisdom, and loss into love.

And that is why this book is not just a narrative of survival—it is a manual for the soul. It teaches us that scars are not meant to be hidden in shame; they are meant to be carried with pride, because they testify not to defeat, but to endurance.

For me, the most haunting thread is the way he rebuilt from ruins—not for ambition, not for accolades, but for remembrance. For Ankush, whose absence he turned into fuel. For his employees, whom he treated as family. For his daughter, to whom he has handed not just a company, but the philosophy of resilience.

This book is not simply about one man's rise. It is about every human being who has been betrayed, who has lost, who has stumbled and still chosen to rise. It whispers to each of us: *your scars too can shine.*

And when you close the final page, as I did, you may find yourself not just admiring Samarth, but also looking inward—asking yourself what scars you carry, and how you might let them light your path instead of darkening it.

With admiration, with humility, and with tears, I commend this book to you. May it open your heart, as it opened mine. May it remind you that the truest monuments in life are not built of stone or steel, but of resilience, remembrance, and love.

—Dr Bina Biswas

MA (English), PhD (English Literature), Delhi

Prologue

A Life Etched in Scars, A Story of Rising Again-Samarth

Every life tells a story. Some are spoken in triumph, some whispered in silence, others carried quietly in shadows. Mine is written in scars.

Scars, I have learnt , are not the handwriting of weakness. They are the stubborn proof of survival. They are the ink with which life scribbles its lessons onto our skin, reminding us that we are often stronger than we ever dared to believe.

I have walked through storms that stripped me bare. I have carried grief heavy enough to bend me to the ground. I have stumbled under the weight of expectations and sat in the hollow silence of loss where no words could reach. Yet, whenever I thought the road had ended, some fragile but insistent voice inside whispered: rise again. And somehow—I did.

Scars That Shape, Not Shatter

Scars come in many disguises. Some are carved by failure, when the world says you are not enough. Some are left by loneliness, when you stand unseen in a room full of people. And some are cut deepest by love—when you have loved so fiercely that its absence leaves an ache in every breath.

My own scars carry all of these stories.

The scar of being the boy who stumbled in classrooms but discovered a fire he did not know he had.

The scar of leaving home and learning freedom in unfamiliar cities.

The scar of building a career, stone by stone, with only determination for mortar.

And the scar of losing someone I loved like a son—a wound that will never close, but one that taught me the raw weight of what it means to truly live.

Each scar has changed me. Not into something broken, but into someone more compassionate, more weathered, more human.

Rising Again

To rise again is not to erase pain. It is to carry it with dignity.

There were nights when grief filled the house like floodwater, when silence was louder than thunder, when the absence of one voice echoed through every room. In those nights, I discovered that healing is not forgetting. Healing is honouring.

So I chose to honour.

To honour love by building.

To honour memory by creating.

To honour life by refusing to let sorrow name me.

Work became my anchor, purpose my compass. Slowly, painfully, beautifully—I rose again.

Success Reimagined

For years, I thought success lived in numbers: the width of a pay cheque, the applause in a hall, the weight of a title. But scars altered my vision.

Today, success is something gentler, more enduring:

- Success is coming home to your daughter's laughter.
- Success is knowing your work has helped children learn, dream, and hope.
- Success is kindness, because you know how cruelty feels.
- Success is daring to love again, even after loss, because love is the only thing that outlives us.

The world may weigh you in wealth, in fame, in power. But when life tests you, you discover what I did:

the true measure of success is not how high you climb, but how deeply you survive.

A Story Meant to Be Shared

Why write this book? Why peel open wounds for strangers to see?

Because scars are not meant to be hidden. They are meant to be lanterns for others still walking in the dark.

This book is not only mine. It belongs to every person who has been told they were not enough and yet kept moving. To every parent who has lost and yet kept loving. To every dreamer who stumbled and yet kept walking.

It is for anyone who has felt broken and still longs to believe that brokenness can become beauty.

The Whisper of Hope

When I stand at my office window and watch the city rush below me, I no longer rush with it. I stand still—with the weight of scars on my shoulders, and the quiet light of resilience in my chest.

I remember the restless boy in Ranchi, the dreamer in Delhi, the young man in Lucknow. And I smile at the man I became: tested, weathered, scarred, yet still standing. A man who, time and again, chose to rise.

And I whisper the same truth to you, dear reader:

You will be scarred. Life will mark you. But scars are not the end of your story. They are the beginning of your strength.

This is not just my story. It is not just one man's journey. It is an invitation—to rise again, no matter how many times life bends you low.

Because if my scars can become my strength, so can yours.

—***Santosh***

Chapter 1

Childhood in Ranchi: The Fire Born from Failure

Ranchi, the capital of Jharkhand, was a city of contradictions. The red earth carried the stubbornness of tribal roots and the coal-rich soil whispered of industry and ambition. Yet families like Samarth's lived in another world altogether—a bubble shaped by discipline, education, and the sharp edge of expectation.

Samarth was the youngest of four—three brothers and a sister—born into what neighbours called a "progressive family." In those days, "progressive" meant the children were sent to good schools, the mother's dignity was guarded, and the father's word carried the weight of final judgment.

But being the youngest was both a gift and a curse. Samarth often felt invisible, like a faint star swallowed by the brilliance of others. His brothers had already earned their badges—discipline, responsibility—and his sister was praised for her obedience. Samarth was restless, curious, too alive to stay contained. Everyone said he was intelligent, but intelligence without discipline, in his father's eyes, was not brilliance at all. It was arrogance.

A Boy Who Would Not Sit Still

From his earliest days in school, Samarth resisted the neat little boxes into which children were pressed. Teachers admired his quick grasp of lessons but scolded his wandering attention, his refusal to sit still, his eyes fixed on the world outside the window as if it called to him louder than chalk on the board.

His mother shielded him as best she could. "He is different," she would tell the neighbours with quiet pride. "He will find his own way." But his father was a man of iron rules and hard results. In his world, marks were the currency of worth, and anything less than excellence was disgrace.

When Samarth scraped through Grade 10 with a dreaded second division, the report card fell on the dining table like a verdict. His father's silence that evening was worse than anger. Later, when the words came, they cracked like thunder across the room:

"You are wasting your life, Samarth. Do you think the world will wait for you? Do you think charm and excuses will feed you? You shame me."

The words seared into Samarth's chest. That night, on a thin cotton mattress beneath the whining ceiling fan, he felt humiliation as something alive, gnawing at him. The house slept, but Samarth lay awake, tears sliding into his pillow, the air thick with failure. For the first time in his life, he understood the sheer weight of expectation, the suffocating grip of judgment.

But in that storm of shame and silence, a strange fire took root—a fire that whispered not of surrender, but of rising.

The Unexpected Victory

The following year, everything changed. Samarth's evenings of cricket in the lane gave way to evenings of scribbling equations under a dim lamp. The glow spilled across his desk while the rest of the house slept.

"Sleep, Samarth!" his mother would call from the other room. But he would mutter to himself, *"Just one more problem... one more."*

Science, the very subject that made his friends groan became his battleground. He no longer ran from it. He attacked it. Formulas that once slipped from his memory were now etched into his notebooks like scars earned in combat.

The morning of the results, his heart pounded

louder than the ticking clock. When the teacher handed him the report card, his hands trembled. *First Division. With Distinction.* Samarth blinked, rubbed his eyes, looked again. *This can't be mine.* He flipped the sheet to check the name. It was his.

At home, he laid the report card on the table. His father, usually brisk and reserved, picked it up. For a long moment, silence filled the room. Samarth's heart raced. Then, slowly, his father looked at him with something Samarth had never seen before-pride, mingled with surprise.

"Well done," his father said quietly, almost as though the words cost him effort. But to Samarth, they were worth more than gold. His mother broke into tears of joy, pressing sweets into his hand.

Samarth smiled. This was not just about numbers on a page. It was about a boy who chose to fight his own shadows, about laughter turned into respect, about doubts turned into dignity. For the first time, Samarth felt not just successful, but unshakably strong.

Teaching Others, Discovering Himself

It began almost by accident. One afternoon, a classmate leaned over during study hour and whispered, "Samarth, can you explain this? I don't get it." Samarth hesitated, then took the chalk and walked up to the board. What started as a simple explanation of a physics law soon turned into something more. He didn't just repeat what the book said-he turned the abstract into stories: currents became rushing rivers, electrons became restless children, formulas became puzzles waiting to be solved.

Before long, a small circle of classmates began gathering around him after school. "Samarth, can you show me that trick again?" "Samarth, how do you remember these formulas?" His evenings, once silent battles with textbooks, now became sessions where laughter and learning mixed freely. He discovered that teaching was not a burden, it was a mirror. With every concept he explained, he understood it more deeply himself.

There was a quiet pride in watching eyes light up—the moment confusion melted into clarity. One of his closest friends, who once dreaded mathematics, began to score above average. Another, who had nearly abandoned physics in despair, went on to secure admission in a reputed engineering college in Ranchi. Those late-night tutoring sessions at Samarth's desk—where the lamp glowed stubbornly and pages rustled like restless wings—became invisible stepping stones to someone else's future.

And yet irony lingered in the room like a shadow

that refused to leave. Here was the boy who had barely scraped through exams, now shaping the victories of others. Sometimes, when the house had gone quiet and he leaned back in his chair, he allowed himself a wry smile at the absurdity of it all. *How strange life is,* he thought. The one once doubted, scolded, and written off was now the one others trusted to lead them forward.

But in that irony lay a truth he could no longer deny. He was not merely intelligent; he was a builder. A builder of confidence. A builder of curiosity. A builder of futures that shone brighter than his own. And in lifting others, Samarth was slowly discovering the hardest, strongest part of himself—the fire born from failure, burning steady against the darkness.

Delhi Did Not Just Open Doors

Delhi did not just open doors for Samarth—it flung the gates wide, daring him to step into a life he had only imagined from afar. Ranchi had given him roots, yes, but Delhi gave him wings and a sky vast enough to test them.

The capital city was intoxicating, almost overwhelming at first. Connaught Place with its glowing neon signs, Janpath alive with bargaining voices, and India Gate shimmering like a monument carved out of light—all became the backdrop of his unfolding story. For a boy who had once stared out of school windows longing for more, Delhi was the answer to a prayer he never dared to say aloud.

For the first time, Samarth tasted anonymity. In Ranchi, he was always "the youngest son of a respected family," his identity sealed by surname and expectation. But in Delhi, swallowed by the chaos of traffic, students, and noise, he was simply Samarth—free to stumble, to experiment, to create himself anew.

He began to walk differently, with the rhythm of a man who belonged. His crisp shirts and polished shoes gave him the confidence of a young professional rather than a hesitant student. With mirrored sunglasses perched on his nose and a notebook tucked neatly under his arm, he looked less like a boy learning to live, more like a man ready to conquer whatever world opened next.

The Carefree Charm

Samarth was never the studious bookworm, but in Delhi, he discovered another strength—his effortless charisma. Professors might not have remembered him for his grades, but classmates remembered his wit, his ability to slip humour into the driest of lectures, turning boredom into laughter.

Girls noticed too. On bus rides, he gave up his seat without hesitation, earning shy glances that lingered longer than the journey. At the canteen, he was the storyteller, spinning ordinary moments into tales that made people laugh until their stomachs hurt. And when he leaned casually against a wall, humming some half-forgotten tune, hands deep in his pockets, it was hard not to look twice.

He wasn't chasing admiration—it came to him uninvited. His carefree confidence did the work on its own.

A Casanova in the Making

There were crushes—fleeting, ridiculous, but memorable all the same. A girl with neat braids who sat beside him in class, scribbling notes so fast it looked as though her pen was running for a bus. Samarth often wondered if she ever read what she wrote or if she simply enjoyed the sound of furious ink. Then there was a senior who bent over his notebook one afternoon and declared, "Your handwriting could be printed on greeting cards." Samarth smiled politely, though in his head he thought, Great, I'll feed my family by writing 'Happy Birthday' a thousand times. The neighbour was the funniest of them all—forever arriving with a stack of papers and an expression of crisis. "Just one small doubt," she'd say, batting her eyelashes. Samarth always helped, of course, though part of him suspected she knew the answers all along. If she keeps inventing doubts like this, she'll qualify for a PhD in excuses, he told himself.

One afternoon, walking toward the bus stop with a classmate, their shoulders brushed. Neither shifted. Their conversation stuttered, like a radio losing signal, before giving way to silence. Samarth could feel his pulse thumping harder than the overloaded DTC bus that rattled past them. He glanced sideways once, then quickly looked ahead. Say something, he urged himself, anything—weather, politics, even cricket scores. But nothing came. Instead, the silence stretched, full of a charge he couldn't name. Later that night, replaying the walk in his head, he muttered, Brilliant, Samarth. Physics may confuse you, but apparently silence is your new language of love.

Another evening, at a college fest, a group of girls dared him to dance. Samarth put up token resistance. "Me? Dance? I can't even walk in a straight line without tripping." The crowd hooted until he gave in. He stepped onto the stage, first with mock clumsiness—two left feet, exaggerated stumbles—earning laughter. Then, almost against his own will, the rhythm caught him. He moved with ease, shoulders loose, smile confident, feet keeping time as if they'd known the beat all along. The crowd roared. By the end, he wasn't just another student blending into the blur of Delhi youth—he was Samarth, the boy who could turn a dare into a memory, who discovered that presence was a kind of performance, and humour was as magnetic as style.

Delhi Nights

The city itself seemed to conspire in his education. Nights in Delhi had a rhythm of their own, a mix of noise and intimacy that Ranchi had never known. Samarth would stroll through Connaught Place long after the shops had shut, sipping steaming chai from chipped glasses beneath yellow streetlamps that made even cracked pavements glow like stage floors.

There were ice cream evenings at India Gate, too—always with company, sometimes with a girl who laughed so loudly that passers-by turned their heads. But Samarth didn't mind; her laughter carried him along until he was laughing louder still, not caring how foolish they looked. Once, he caught his reflection in the polished side of a parked scooter—cone in hand, face lit by amusement—and thought, *So this is what happiness looks like, sticky fingers and all.*

The buses were their own kind of classroom.

Wedged into the back of an overcrowded DTC, Samarth learnt that conversations didn't need space, only timing. Jokes travelled faster than tickets, and sometimes glances did too—mischievous, fleeting glances exchanged with strangers who smiled back just long enough to leave a mark before melting into the crowd at the next stop. He never asked their names; Delhi taught him that not every connection was meant to last, some were simply meant to spark.

Delhi nights were stitched together with this strange magic that belonged only to the young. A cool breeze across Janpath, carrying dust and perfume in equal measure. The smoky scent of roasted corn curling upward from street vendors, mingling with the blare of rickshaw horns. The echo of laughter bouncing between buildings, refusing to die out. It was messy, noisy, sometimes exhausting—but all of it wrapped Samarth in a cloak of endless possibility, the feeling that every street corner could turn into a story, and every night could be the beginning of something new.

Not Just a Lover, But a Listener

What made Samarth different was that he wasn't reckless. For him, attraction wasn't conquest, and charm was never a weapon. He listened. He remembered the small details—how someone liked their chai, which exam worried them most, the song they hummed when they thought no one noticed. He treated every smile, every secret shared, as something rare.

Women trusted him not because he was flawless, but because with him they felt seen. He carried himself like a Casanova, but without arrogance or hunger. His charm wasn't just in polished shoes and confident smiles, but in warmth—the kind that lingered long after he walked away.

He didn't collect girlfriends. He collected moments. A rickshaw ride under flickering streetlights. A joke shared in the hush of a library. A lingering goodbye at the gate, where words ran out but glances spoke volumes.

Delhi Nights, Ranchi Shadows

Delhi dazzled Samarth with its lights, its markets, its endless invitations to be someone new. Connaught Place and India Gate were playgrounds of laughter, late-night tea, and whispered possibilities. Yet even as the city conspired in his education, shadows from Ranchi travelled with him, stubborn as the red earth he had left behind

Back home, his parents oscillated between pride and unease. Pride, because their son was in Delhi, shaping a life from sheer determination. Worry, because Samarth had always been restless, unpredictable—a boy whose moods and silences could not be tamed by rules. At first, there were letters filled with careful lines, phone calls where his mother fussed over meals and his father demanded proof of progress. But as months thickened into years, the words dwindled. The letters grew fewer, the calls shorter, and silence settled in—not the silence of peace, but of absence.

His siblings, too, were swallowed by their own ambitions. At family gatherings, Samarth was both present and absent. Present when they said, "At least he's surviving in Delhi." Absent when, with subtle smiles sharper than blades, they added, "But what has he really achieved?" Samarth's charm deflected their words—he smiled, laughed, nodded—but the laughter never reached his chest. Inside, he carried loneliness like a shadow no one else could see.

And so Delhi became two cities for him: one where he was Samarth the charmer, the dancer, the teller of jokes; and another, quieter Delhi, where he lay awake at night in his small rented room, staring at the ceiling fan, wondering why even victories felt tinged with an ache he couldn't name.

Reflection in the Midst of Noise

Looking back, Samarth would say Ranchi had taught him pain and pride in equal measure. Pain, because he had always felt misunderstood—the boy who gave quietly but was rarely seen, who learned that even in families, love could be conditional. Pride, because in that same soil of dismissals, his resilience had taken root. Every overlooked gesture, every subtle comparison, became a stone in the foundation he was building for himself.

He carried two truths like secret talismans:

That affection could be rationed, like inheritance.

That his worth would never be handed down; it would have to be carved, stone by stone, with his own hands.

And so, as Delhi nights wrapped him in laughter, roasted corn smoke, and mischievous glances from strangers, Ranchi's silence never left him. It was the furnace where his fire had been lit—the reminder that no matter how many smiled at his jokes or admired his confidence, he had to keep proving himself, not just to the world, but to the boy who once lay awake on a thin mattress, burning with the sting of his father's words.

Chapter 2

The Turning Point – Delhi & Early Struggles

Leaving for Delhi

When Samarth boarded the train to Delhi, he wasn't just leaving Ranchi; he was stepping into an unknown life. The boy who had always been called the "youngest son" was now chasing his own horizon.

The train rattled through forests, fields, and towns, carrying him toward a city of opportunity. Samarth pressed his face against the window, eyes wide, as the scenery shifted—mud huts giving way to concrete houses, sleepy villages blooming into restless towns. Every turn of the wheel seemed to whisper: your future is waiting.

Inside the compartment, strangers became companions. An elderly couple unpacked a tiffin of fragrant biryani and insisted he try it. Samarth, with his easy charm, accepted and soon had them laughing with stories of street cricket in Ranchi, mimicking bowlers and neighbourhood quarrels with comic exaggeration.

Across the aisle, two college girls wrestled with heavy bags, their laughter rising with every failed attempt to push them onto the rack. Samarth saw his chance.

"Allow me," he said, giving a mock bow before flexing far more than necessary as he hoisted the bags effortlessly.

"Impressive," one of them teased, her eyes sparkling.

"Years of practice," Samarth replied, brushing imaginary dust off his shirt. "You'd be surprised how heavy cricket kits can be."

The ice was broken. Soon they were swapping jokes, sharing snacks, debating which café in Delhi had the best sandwiches. At one point, he noticed one girl shivering under the breeze from the open window. He offered his jacket, saying softly, "Delhi nights can be unpredictable." She half-smiled, half-blushed, and her friend teased, "Well, looks like someone found a Delhi gentleman before reaching Delhi."

Samarth laughed with them, but inside he felt something new—an unexpected thrill, a sense of belonging among strangers. For the first time, he wasn't just someone's younger brother or the restless boy from Ranchi. He was Samarth: storyteller, helper, dreamer, perhaps even a little bit of a charmer.

The rhythm of the wheels, the warmth of conversation, and the sparkle of innocent flirtation made the journey feel almost magical. Delhi wasn't just a destination. It was liberation.

Delhi: The City of Smoke and Dreams

Delhi greeted him like a tidal wave. Blaring horns, screeching autos, swirling dust, the aromas of street food curling through the air, and the restless energy of ambition all crashed into him at once. For someone from Ranchi, where life moved slower and faces were familiar, the capital felt like stepping into another universe.

Samarth stayed with his elder brother in a modest flat. His brother, practical and disciplined, became his first anchor in the storm, guiding him through admissions, paperwork, and the bewildering bureaucracy of a big city. With his help, Samarth secured a seat at a reputable college. It wasn't Delhi's most elite institution, but it was a beginning—and for Samarth, beginnings mattered more than names carved on gates.

This was more than his brother's support. It was his family's silent faith in him. Even from a distance, every gesture reminded him: though he had left Ranchi behind, he carried their hopes like invisible luggage, heavier than any bag hoisted onto a train rack.

College Life: More Than Books

Walking onto the campus, Samarth felt a quiet pride. He had made it to Delhi, and that alone was a small victory carved from years of doubt. The classrooms, professors, and exams were part of the routine, but for Samarth they were never the whole story.

While many students memorised notes and chased grades with mechanical precision, Samarth's mind wandered elsewhere. He rephrased ideas in his own words, tested them against experience, and questioned what others accepted blindly. His marks hovered in the middle range—neither a disaster nor a triumph—but his originality marked him out.

Professors often shook their heads with the same remark: "This boy has spark. If only he channels it." Samarth smiled to himself when he heard it. He knew his real education was not happening inside lecture halls—it was taking place outside, in the city that demanded as much resilience as any textbook.

Learning the City, Learning Himself

Delhi itself became his greatest teacher. He learnt to stretch five rupees through the day, to board overcrowded buses without being flattened, to smile politely even while bargaining with shopkeepers who doubled prices the moment they saw he was new. Each lesson toughened him, each failure shaped him, each small victory sharpened him for the next.

But college brought bruises too. He still remembered the sting of sitting in a seminar when a wealthy classmate smirked at his scuffed shoes and whispered loud enough for others to hear, "Small-town boy, big-city dreams." The laughter that followed burned hotter than any reprimand from his father ever had. Samarth smiled it away, but inside he promised himself he would never again let someone mistake simplicity for weakness.

And there were moments that healed. On another afternoon, struggling with the cost of a second-hand book he desperately needed, Samarth found the shopkeeper quietly slip it into his bag, saying only, "Pay me when you can." That small kindness stayed with him longer than any insult, proof that the city wasn't only about smoke and survival—it had room for unexpected grace too.

Evenings often carried their own kind of magic. Samarth would drift through Connaught Place, its white colonnades glowing beneath neon signs, its pavements alive with a restless hum—vendors calling out, couples strolling with linked hands, office workers hurrying home, each life rushing past his. Sometimes he sat on a bench with nothing but the night breeze and the crowd for company, observing quietly. Nobody knew him here; nobody compared him with anyone. In that anonymity, he felt a kind of freedom Ranchi had never allowed him.

And yet, Delhi never quite erased Ranchi. He carried fragments of home like a private inheritance—the smell of his mother's cooking, his father's pipe smoke curling in the evening air, the playful chatter of siblings during power cuts when candles cast long shadows across the room. These memories weren't burdens; they were roots. They reminded him of where he had begun, and gave him strength as he stumbled, learnt, and slowly carved a new path through Delhi's chaos.

A Glimpse of Charm

Samarth was not just learning academics—he was discovering himself, almost against his own impatience. Tall, sharp-featured, restless, he carried a charm that seemed to arrive uninvited. His smile broke tensions in classrooms, his jokes made even dull lectures bearable, and when he listened—really listened—people found themselves saying more than they had intended.

Girls noticed. Samarth noticed too, though always with a certain restraint that baffled even himself. *Why do I stop here? Why not take the leap?* he sometimes thought, then brushed the question aside. One girl in particular caught his eye—the one with the braid that slid over her shoulder like a dark rope of silk. Her notes were always neat, her voice soft but firm, her discipline unbending.

They exchanged books. They laughed over scribbled margins. They often walked together to the bus stop, where the neem trees threw shadows across the road and the air smelt of dust and fried snacks.

"Why do you always smile when you hand me your notebook?" she teased once, raising her eyebrows.

"Because your handwriting deserves a smile," Samarth replied with a mock bow. Inside, though, his chest tightened at the simplicity of her glance, the way her eyes widened when surprised—as though the whole world had just startled her.

There were days he wanted to say more. Words perched on his lips like birds ready to fly, but something in him pulled back. Attraction, he believed, wasn't about racing forward—it was about letting moments stretch, about lingering in the silence after a joke, about the accidental brush of fingers when both reached for the same book.

And yet, when evenings fell and the crowd thinned, loneliness sometimes caught up with him. Sitting alone in his small room, with the ceiling fan groaning above and the moonlight creeping through half-shut curtains, he whispered to himself: You are not collecting girlfriends, Samarth. You are collecting memories.

First Job: A Taste of Responsibility

When college ended, reality barged in like an uninvited guest that refused to leave. A degree sat proudly in his hand, but his pockets were hollow. Nights of wandering Connaught Place and laughing at bus stops gave way to the silence of decisions.

"Further studies?" he muttered, pacing in his room. "And who will pay the fees, Samarth? Dreams don't come on credit." His reflection in the dusty mirror stared back at him, unsparing.

Responsibility spoke louder than longing. His family needed support, he craved independence, and there was a quiet thrill in the thought of standing on his own feet at last. Opportunity came through educational publishing—a modest role in the sales department. Sales. The very word made him frown. Sales? Is that what I came to Delhi for? To hawk books like vegetables?

But when he walked into the interview, his doubt melted into resolve. He didn't speak like a nervous graduate fumbling for chances. He spoke like a young man who had decided to take life head-on. He talked about discipline, about hunger to prove himself, about his willingness to learn. The panel, expecting hesitation, instead found fire.

"You're sure you want sales?" one interviewer asked, leaning back sceptically.

Samarth looked him in the eye. "I want responsibility. You can call it what you like."

They hired him.

The first pay cheque he held felt heavier than paper had any right to feel. His palms tingled as though he was holding not money, but dignity itself. He sent gifts home—small but thoughtful: a soft saree for his mother, a sturdy pen for his father, a toy that made his little nephew shriek with joy. For himself, he chose freedom on two wheels: a black motorcycle, sleek and fast, its chrome catching the morning sun. That machine didn't just carry him from home to office—it carried him into youth. It took him to late-night chai stalls where steam curled into the night sky, down sunlit highways that smelt of dust and wildflowers, into roads that whispered of endless possibilities.

Yet, beneath the exhilaration lay exhaustion. The days were long, the targets relentless, the city indifferent. At times, sitting alone with his helmet at his side, he muttered in exasperation: "So this is what growing up feels like? Deadlines instead of dreams, silence instead of applause." But then the night breeze would brush his face, the trees along the highway would sway like witnesses, and he would remember—this was only the beginning.

Even as he built his career, the hunger for learning never left him. Years later, he enrolled in a management programme, burning midnight oil over books after returning from sales trips. By day he battled numbers, by night he sharpened ideas. He was no longer just a salesman; he was shaping himself for leadership, proving that ambition could walk two roads at once—career and education—if one had the stamina to keep moving.

That first job, with its modest desk and ordinary title, became his rite of passage. It taught him what no classroom could: resilience, responsibility, and the fierce pride of self-earned success. It wasn't just a pay cheque. It was the first bold stroke in the larger story of a life determined never to be ordinary.

Lucknow: The City of Nawabs, The City of Freedom

Samarth's job posting took him to Lucknow, a city slower than Delhi, yet alive with poetry. Its wide boulevards carried the fragrance of kebabs and ittar, its Mughal arches whispered of lost empires, and its evenings glowed with the warmth of shayari echoing in weathered courtyards. In the haze of twilight, when pigeons wheeled above domes and the Gomti breeze drifted across the city, Samarth realised this was not just a transfer; it was an immersion into a culture where history and romance still danced hand in hand.

Here, life found a new rhythm. His office routine gave him structure, but it was his black motorcycle that gave him wings. Cutting through leafy avenues where Gul mohar trees burnt scarlet in the summer, he felt both independent and limitless. At roadside tea stalls, amidst steaming glasses of cutting chai, the crackle of pakoras, and bursts of laughter, friendships blossomed with an ease Delhi had never offered. Lucknow, he learnt, was not a place to rush—it was a place to savour, to breathe slowly, to let time slip through your fingers like poetry recited under the stars.

Women noticed him too. Perhaps it was the easy confidence in his stride, or the way his eyes didn't just look but listened, or maybe the balance he carried between charm and restraint. There were strolls down Hazrat Ganj under glowing lamplight, long conversations tucked into the quiet corners of bookshops where the scent of old pages mingled with fresh ink, and the thrill of late-evening chaat, the tang of tamarind clinging to laughter. Yet Samarth always drew the line with respect. His attraction never dissolved into recklessness; it was careful, dignified, and that restraint gave him a gravity others admired.

Once, when a colleague hesitated to ride home alone after a late meeting, Samarth swung his bike into gear and followed her until she turned safely into her lane. Another evening, during a canteen gathering, someone dared him to recite poetry. Smiling, he quoted a few lines of Urdu, the syllables rolling soft and steady. The girls clapped, laughing, "Samarth, you sound more like a Lucknowi shayaar than a Ranchi boy or Delhi boy!" He laughed with them, embarrassed yet secretly pleased—because in that moment, he wasn't just living in the city, he was absorbing its soul.

Colleagues often teased him.

"Samarth bhai, you're a hero!" they'd grin, watching how he balanced work, friendship, and admiration without slipping into arrogance.

But Samarth knew it wasn't heroism. It was balance. Lucknow had taught him what Delhi never did—that freedom wasn't about running wild, it was about living with grace. In the slow afternoons where sunlight spread lazily across verandahs, in the star-studded nights when music drifted from hidden courtyards, in the soulful conversations over kebabs and tea, he learnt that responsibility and romance could coexist.

And yet, there were nights when silence pressed harder than noise. In his rented room, with only the whir of a ceiling fan and the glow of a lone bulb, loneliness returned like an old companion. The laughter of friends faded as doors shut, the city's bustle softened into distant echoes, and Samarth lay awake, staring at cracked plaster on the ceiling. In those hours, he thought of Ranchi—his mother's voice calling him to dinner, the playful quarrels during power cuts, the familiar scent of home. Lucknow was shaping his heart, yes, but its quietest corners reminded him that roots, once stretched, ache in their absence.

Lucknow didn't just shape his career. It shaped his heart. It taught him that life wasn't only about chasing the horizon—it was also about pausing, listening, and carrying loneliness with dignity, until it turned into strength.

Seeds of Ambition

Professionally, Samarth was beginning to thrive. Sales suited him because it was about people, not just numbers. He connected, persuaded, explained—not with rehearsed pitches, but with sincerity that disarmed even the most sceptical principals. Bookstore owners welcomed him with tea, colleagues leaned on his energy, and soon managers began to notice.

"This young man," one remarked during a review, "has more than drive—he has vision."

Samarth realised he wasn't simply selling books. He was spreading knowledge, planting seeds that might one day blossom in classrooms he would never see. That thought changed something inside him. It made him ambitious—not hungry for status alone, but for purpose.

Job switches followed, each one like a rung on a ladder. They weren't reckless leaps, but careful, deliberate climbs. Each move polished him sharper, widened his network, and added weight to his reputation. Unlike many peers, he never drifted into glamorous industries. Publishing, to him, was more than trade—it was a calling.

Foreign offers arrived in shiny envelopes—Dubai, Singapore, even London. Salaries sparkled, perks dazzled, futures promised ease. Friends urged him: "Samarth, why hesitate? The world is waiting."

But he shook his head, a quiet stubbornness in his tone. "My world is here. If I rise here, I rise with meaning." His refusal puzzled some, but for Samarth the choice was clear. India's children, its schools and libraries, were the soil in which his ambition had to grow.

Reflection

Delhi had been his turning point. It gave him independence, the courage to step out of his comfort zone, anonymity that allowed him to make mistakes without judgement, and survival skills that toughened him for life's storms. In its fast lanes and crowded streets, he learnt how to stand tall, how to carve out space in a world that never stopped moving.

Lucknow, by contrast, gave him roots and responsibility. Its leafy boulevards taught him patience, its courtyards whispered history, its people balanced grace with discipline. Lucknow refined his ambition, gave structure to his scattered energy, and reminded him that freedom always carries the weight of accountability.

Together, the two cities sculpted him into a man who could climb ladders with both confidence and grace. Delhi gave him wings; Lucknow gave him an anchor. One taught him to rise, the other to stay grounded. Together, they turned uncertainty into purpose.

The Man Emerging

The boy from Ranchi, who once felt ordinary and overlooked, now found himself transforming into someone extraordinary—stylish in his presence, ambitious in his pursuits, brimming with dreams too large for silence. Yet loneliness never left him fully; it lingered at the edges of late evenings, when even applause from colleagues faded into quiet. In those hours, he would sit by a window, the night breeze carrying the smell of dust and distant rain, and whisper to himself: *You are moving forward. Do not forget where you began.*

Every step forward was stitched with the blessings of home. His parents' unwavering love, his brother's steady support, and the warmth of Ranchi's roots remained the invisible foundation beneath his journey. They reminded him that while ambition could propel him forward, it was gratitude that kept him steady.

And so, he walked on—a dreamer shaped by three cities, a man forged by love, loneliness, and hope.

Chapter 3

First Job, First Love, and the Style of a Young Man in Lucknow

Arrival in Lucknow

Lucknow was not Ranchi, and it was not Delhi. It stood somewhere between the two—refined yet restless, rooted in history yet hungry for change. Its wide boulevards carried the fragrance of kebabs and ittar, its Mughal arches whispered of lost empires, and its evenings glowed with the music of shayari echoing in old courtyards where time seemed reluctant to move forward.

For Samarth, it became a stage, a school, and a testing ground. The publishing house he joined was modest, a cluster of plain rooms with overstuffed cupboards and rattling fans. But to him, it was another universe. For the first time, he had a desk with his name neatly printed on a brass plate, carried an official designation, and received a salary folded carefully into an envelope.

The day he held his first pay cheque, his hands trembled. It wasn't much, but to him it was more than money—it was freedom, it was proof. That evening, alone in his small flat, he pressed it against his chest and whispered: "You've done it, Samarth." Then the whisper faded into silence, and a pang cut through him: there was no one there to witness the moment. Still, he sent money home, bought his mother a soft saree, his father a sturdy pen, sweets for neighbours who had once doubted him. For himself, he bought something that would define his youth forever: a motorcycle.

The Bike: Freedom on Wheels

The day Samarth bought his motorcycle, something inside him shifted. It wasn't just a machine—it was an extension of his spirit, a declaration that the boy from Ranchi had grown into a man who could command attention.

Every Sunday morning, before the city fully stirred, he polished it until the chrome gleamed like liquid silver. The sun caught on the handlebars, flashing into the eyes of curious neighbours. "Samarth bhai, Lucknow ka hero ban gaye ho!" they teased. And in truth, he was—for when the engine roared to life, it wasn't only the bike that came alive, but Samarth's heart too.

On that bike, he shed the skin of the overlooked younger son. The wind lashed against his face, his mirrored sunglasses caught the city's lights, and every turn of the wheel whispered: *freedom*.

But the bike was not just glamour—it was romance. It carried stolen moments and secret journeys.

There were office evenings when a colleague, tired of fluorescent lights and endless files, climbed onto the pillion seat. They rode into the night, their laughter cutting through the traffic, the city slipping away until only the hum of the engine and the promise of escape remained. Her dupatta fluttered like a flag of rebellion as she leaned closer, whispering secrets into the rushing wind.

There were female acquaintances who asked for "just one round" after coffee, and one round always turned into long rides past the city borders. The bookstore girl clutched him tightly on moonlit roads, her braid brushing against his shoulder, her heartbeat quickening with every acceleration. The shy neighbour leaned gently against his back, her cheek resting between his shoulder blades, the city lights shimmering in her wide eyes. And the bold one? She laughed wildly, her hair whipping loose, urging him to go faster—to race the wind itself.

Some nights belonged only to the highway. The

stretch between Lucknow and Kanpur became his stage—seventy-five kilometres of darkness and wild forest, where the headlight carved a silver path into mystery. The trees whispered overhead, shadows danced at the edges, and every turn felt like a secret rendezvous with destiny. Sometimes, with a female friend holding him tight, the silence of the forest turned intimate—the world reduced to the hum of the engine, the beating of two hearts, and the daring romance of riding into the unknown.

Those rides were not just journeys; they were dangerous poems written in speed and shadows. The forest stretched endlessly, its stillness broken only by the throaty roar of the engine. The moon hung like a watchful guardian, casting silver light on her face as she rested against his shoulder. Every time the bike leaned into a curve, it felt as though they were tilting into another world—one where fear and thrill blended seamlessly into desire. The darkness was thick, yet her laughter rang like a bell, making the night feel alive. The 75 km stretch wasn't only a road; it was a lover's corridor, where the thrill of danger made every touch electric, every breath shared under the canopy of stars unforgettable.

Rain-soaked evenings when they pulled under trees, their laughter mingling with raindrops. Early dawns when he drove through empty streets, arms looped around his waist, a head nestled against him in trust. Evenings when the bike waited faithfully outside cinema halls, the thrill of the film paling beside the electric warmth of her hand slipping into his.

The motorcycle became his stage, his spotlight, his silent companion. Long after its metal dulled, the memories remained polished in his heart. For Samarth, it wasn't only freedom on wheels—it was the rhythm of youth, the backdrop of first loves, the vessel that carried both joy and loneliness through the labyrinth of early manhood.

The Bookstore Girl

It began in the aisles of a small Lucknow bookstore. Samarth stopped there often on his way back from work, flipping through titles more out of habit than need. That's when he noticed her—a girl with long braids, her dupatta slipping loose as she arranged piles of books. Her eyes lingered on him a moment too long before darting away.

At first, their words were light. She recommended a poetry collection; he countered with a history book. Slowly, conversations spilled beyond the shop—coffee at a corner café, samosas at a roadside stall, walks along streets glowing with lamplight.

One evening, they rode along the Gomti River. The breeze carried her laughter into the dark, the water glimmered with moonlight. When he stopped under a streetlamp, silence stretched between them. She looked down, her braid slipping forward. Samarth brushed it back gently. In that tender pause, he leant closer.

Their lips met—hesitant, searching, then certain. Her hands clutched his arm as though afraid the moment might dissolve. Around them, the city blurred, the river shimmered, and for a heartbeat the universe was theirs alone.

From then on, kisses came like secrets—hidden in quiet alleys after long rides, or stolen quickly before she stepped into her gate. Sometimes, she held him tightly from behind on the bike, her cheek pressed against his back, her arms circling him with a closeness that spoke louder than words. He could feel her breath against his neck, and it sent a shiver through him every time.

They never rushed. Their love grew in the spaces between words—her fingers grazing his as she handed him a book, his teasing remark that sent colour to her cheeks, the way she leaned into him on rides, head resting lightly against his shoulder. Yet within those small gestures, passion simmered—an intensity that made every glance, every brush of her hand, feel electric.

When she visited his flat once to return a borrowed novel, she quietly straightened his messy stack of papers. He watched from the doorway, struck by how natural it felt to see her there. She turned, caught his gaze, and smiled shyly. That smile was soft fire—gentle, patient, yet burning with a depth he hadn't known before. He stepped closer, unable to resist, and when she lifted her face, their kiss deepened, longer, more certain than before. She rested her forehead against his chest afterwards, and in that embrace, Samarth felt both the fragility and the strength of what bound them together.

But with romance came sadness, a shadow that never quite left Samarth. Nights ended too soon, departures always hurt. Lying awake afterwards, he would listen to the fan whirring, stare at the cracked ceiling, and wonder: How long can this last? Does love in Lucknow carry permanence, or is it another passing fragrance, like ittar fading by dawn?

The ache of that question never left him. For Samarth, she was not just the bookstore girl. She was the poetry of his youth—half song, half silence—the kind of love that lingers even when time moves on.

The Bold One – Love Beyond the Apartment Walls

She was introduced by a colleague, and from the very first

evening, Samarth knew she was different. Bolder, freer, unafraid of closeness. She teased easily, laughed without restraint, and when she looked at him, it was with a frankness that made him both flattered and uneasy. Her love was fiery, yes—but beneath the flame there was a surprising tenderness, a softness that caught him off guard.

Her visits began casually—dropping by to borrow a book, to share leftover food, to tease him about his chaotic apartment. Soon, her presence became habitual. She started tidying his scattered papers, stacking his books into neat piles, humming while she moved about as though she already belonged there. She cooked in his small kitchen, filling it with the smell of cumin sputtering in hot oil, garlic crisping in the pan, rice steaming gently on the stove.

Samarth often leant against the kitchen doorway, watching her.

"You're turning my bachelor flat into a palace," he said one evening, grinning as she stirred a pot.

"Palace?" she scoffed, rolling her eyes. "This is barely a room. But at least it doesn't have to smell like socks all the time."

"Oi!" Samarth protested, laughing. "Those socks have history."

"And bacteria," she shot back, brandishing the ladle like a weapon.

Dinner was never just a meal. It was foreplay disguised as domesticity—the clinking of plates, her mock–scolding about his untidy habits, his hand brushing hers as he reached for a spoon, her quick, daring glance before she turned away. When the food was eaten and the dishes rinsed, they curled up together on the old sofa, sometimes whispering into the night, sometimes losing themselves in passion so fierce it left them trembling.

Over time, her overnight visits became longer. Her dupatta found a place draped on his chair, her anklets jingled softly in his room, her perfume lingered on the pillow beside his. More than once, as dawn broke through the curtains, they held each other close and wished the world outside would wait. It was as if they were already living as husband and wife—sharing mornings, teasing over tea, exchanging long kisses before he left for work, and collapsing into each other's arms at night.

Their intimacy deepened in the rhythm of daily life. She ironed his shirts before important meetings, tied his tie while standing on tiptoe, reminded him to eat when work consumed him, and waited with tea on the table when he returned home exhausted. Once, seeing the weariness in his face, she said simply, "You carry too much on your shoulders, Samarth. Let me carry some of it for you." For him, it was the first taste of what it meant to be truly looked after.

And when passion overcame them, their embraces turned desperate, their kisses long and lingering. They held each other as though afraid the world might tear them apart, their bodies pressed close, every heartbeat a confession. For Samarth, she wasn't just the bold one—she was the woman who made his apartment feel like a home, the woman who blurred the line between romance and family, freedom and belonging.

Romance at the Cinema

Lucknow's single-screen theatres became their sanctuaries. On Friday evenings, they joined the queues of couples, families, and friends, slipping into the dim halls heavy with the smell of popcorn and dust. They shared samosas during intermissions, nudged each other with jokes over loud musical numbers, and laughed far too much at comedies that deserved less.

But the real story unfolded in the dark. During hushed moments when the screen glowed soft blue, their fingers brushed, hesitated, then intertwined. The thrill of sitting so close—the brush of her shoulder, the faint perfume that clung to her shawl—was intoxicating.

Once, during a romantic film, she leaned against him, her head gently resting on his shoulder. Samarth's heart pounded so violently he could barely hear the dialogue. The movie blurred into background noise; the real romance flickered between them in stolen glances, in the electricity of her touch hidden by shadows.

Afterwards, they spilled out into the night air, the streets alive with hawkers, the smell of roasted corn drifting across the pavements. She climbed onto his bike, her arms wrapping around his waist, holding tighter than usual. "Faster," she whispered once, her voice half-challenge, half-laughter, her hair whipping against his cheek. He accelerated, the city lights streaking past, their laughter flying into the dark like sparks.

Yet even in the blaze of their closeness, loneliness sometimes crept in like a shadow at the edges. When the laughter died and she returned to her own world, Samarth found himself staring at the quiet apartment—the cushions she had arranged, the framed picture on the wall, the faint trace of her perfume in the curtains. For a moment it felt like home, but when she wasn't there, it felt emptier than before. That was the paradox of their love: it filled him to overflowing, and it hollowed him out with longing the moment she left.

The Shy Neighbour

She was different from the others—softer, quieter, almost invisible at first. A neighbour who lived across the narrow lane, her presence was always in glimpses: the rustle of bangles when she watered plants on her balcony, the shy smile when their eyes met, the way she adjusted her dupatta when he caught her looking.

At first, their exchanges were no more than nods and polite greetings. But slowly, little moments stitched their story together. She lent him a notebook once when he needed paper. He returned it with a new pen tucked inside. She thanked him, her cheeks flushing, her voice trembling just above a whisper.

Soon, they began walking back from the market together. The first time their shoulders brushed, she startled, then smiled. Samarth noticed how her eyes never held his gaze for long, but her silence carried more than words. She was the kind of girl who spoke with lowered lashes and said yes with the tilt of her head.

Their romance grew in stolen spaces. She would watch him polish his bike, pretending to be busy with something else, until he finally offered her a ride. The first time she climbed onto the seat, her hands hovered nervously before finally circling his waist. That touch, hesitant yet warm, sent a shiver through him.

Evenings became their secret ritual. A short ride after work, the city lights glowing around them, her cheek pressed against his back. She rarely spoke, but her closeness spoke volumes.

One evening, rain began to fall as they rode. He pulled over under a tree. The drizzle blurred the world into silver lines. She laughed nervously, her hair damp, clinging to her face. He reached to tuck a strand behind her ear, and in that moment, the shy neighbour who blushed at every glance leaned into his touch. Their lips met—hesitant at first, then lingering, sweet and slow. The rain hid them, but for them, nothing else existed.

After that, something shifted. She began visiting his flat under small excuses—returning a book, borrowing sugar, asking for help with a bill. But once inside, she would linger, sitting on the edge of the chair, her fingers brushing his tablecloth. He offered her tea, and they sat close, talking in low tones that always trailed into silence.

The silence carried weight. His hand found hers one evening, and she didn't pull away. Another evening, her dupatta slipped slightly, and when he reached to adjust it, his fingers grazed her collarbone. She closed her eyes, not moving, her breath quickening.

Their intimacy was not hurried like with others. It was a slow unravelling—like peeling petals from a rose. A hand held longer than necessary. A head resting on his chest as they listened to the hum of the ceiling fan. A kiss that deepened, gently at first, then with urgency as weeks passed.

And then came the nights where kisses turned wild—where her shyness melted into longing. Her lips trembled against his, only to part willingly as he pulled her closer. She clung to him with surprising strength, as though she never wanted to let go. Their embraces grew longer, their laughter mingling with sighs. She would tease him shyly in whispers, only to blush and bury her face in his chest when he teased back.

In his small flat, they began to act like husband and wife. She folded his laundry, teased him about his unpolished shoes, left her bangles on his table and her scent on his pillow. He loved returning home to find her waiting, the kettle whistling, her eyes lighting up at the sight of him. At night, they curled together on the sofa or the bed, kisses deepening until the world outside ceased to exist. They explored each other slowly, with both innocence and hunger, losing themselves in long embraces that felt both tender and thrilling.

Samarth found himself dreaming of a future with her—not just moments, but years. He wanted to marry this girl, to make her his wife, to keep her laughter, her care, her shy but fierce love beside him forever.

She trusted him with her shyness, and that trust became intoxicating. In her innocence, he discovered a different kind of sensuality—not fiery, but tender, almost sacred. Their love was fragile, but it was also thrilling, precisely because it existed in whispers, in shadows, in the quiet glow of evenings spent together.

For Samarth, she wasn't just a neighbour. She was the soft heartbeat of his Lucknow days—the secret romance that taught him desire doesn't always need fire; sometimes, it blooms in the gentlest touch, in wild kisses that end in laughter, and in the dream of turning passion into permanence.

Lucknow: Lessons in Love and Freedom

Lucknow gave Samarth more than his first job and pay cheque—it gave him freedom. And with freedom came experiences that painted his youth in colours of passion and discovery.

Yet unlike his peers, who boasted of conquests as though they were medals, Samarth carried his adventures quietly, like secret treasures locked away in the heart. He had known different shades of love: the innocent blush of the shy neighbour, the poetry of the bookstore girl, the fiery storm of the bold one. Each had left a mark, not like scars, but like brushstrokes—soft, fierce, unforgettable—shaping him in ways he rarely admitted aloud.

There were evenings of whispered conversations in dim cafés, mornings of laughter over steaming chai at small stalls, afternoons with curtains drawn and hearts racing. There were hands that found his in crowded cinema halls, lips that sought him under rainy skies, and bodies discovering one another in the stillness of shuttered rooms.

But more than passion, what stayed with him was trust. Women trusted him—not because he was flawless, but because he listened, because he respected silences as much as words, boundaries as much as desires.

Once, when a girl rested her head on his shoulder after an argument, she murmured:

"Samarth, I feel safe with you."

And for him, those words meant more than the heat of any kiss.

He had tasted kisses beneath moonlight, felt the steady weight of a woman's head on his chest as she drifted into sleep, shared meals cooked in his bare bachelor kitchen transformed by a woman's touch. Each moment added spice to his freedom—not just in passion, but in tenderness.

Often, when the day's noise had faded, Samarth stood at his balcony. Above him, the sky turned dusky, streaked with violet and gold. Lonely birds wheeled back to their nests, their wings dark silhouettes against the fading light. From a neighbour's kitchen, the aroma of frying onions and spices drifted through the air, mingling with the damp smell of earth after sprinklers had soaked the garden below. He would close his eyes, inhale, and realise: these were the moments that made him. Not the deals signed at work, not the teasing of colleagues, but these quiet recognitions that he was living, feeling, becoming.

And so the realisation dawned—what made him different was not charm alone. It was remembrance. While others flaunted, he reflected. While others chased numbers, he cherished bonds. His romances were not trophies, but lessons—teaching him that true grace lay not in how many hearts you won, but in how gently you held the ones that chose you.

Yet, in those twilight hours, another truth flickered at the edges of his mind—a truth he tried to push aside. Birds returned to their nests, but not all nests remained whole. Perfume lingered in the air, but only until dawn. Love, he sensed, was never his to keep forever; it was only his to honour while it lasted. A shadow crept into his freedom, whispering that every embrace was also a goodbye in disguise.

That was the fiery, tender side of his freedom—not to roam endlessly, but to discover love in all its forms: laughter, silence, fire, and warmth. And yet, already, Lucknow was preparing him for the ache that follows joy, the loneliness that seeps in after doors close, the scars that passion inevitably leaves behind.

Work and Play

While nights overflowed with tenderness, days marched under the banner of ambition.

Samarth excelled in sales because he understood people. He listened where others pressed, explained where others pushed. Principals trusted him, bookstore owners welcomed him, colleagues leaned on him. His reputation grew—not just as someone who closed deals, but as someone who inspired trust.

Lucknow was shaping him—not into a braggart, not into a restless wanderer—but into a man of charm, depth, and direction. And in the twilight hours, as birds disappeared into shadows and the world smelt of suppers being prepared, he learnt to whisper to himself: *This, too, is what it means to live.*

But somewhere deep down, he also sensed: *This, too, will not last.*

The Shift after Marriage

When marriage finally came, it was not just an event—it was a turning point. Friends teased him mercilessly: "Ab toh hero settle ho gaya! Bike se utar kar family man ban gaye ho." (Now the hero is off the bike and has become a family man.)

They pictured the end of late-night rides, whispered cinema kisses, and carefree evenings spent idling under streetlamps. Samarth only laughed. For them, marriage was a cage; for him, it felt like a compass pointing towards something greater.

His wife was not loud or flamboyant. She carried herself with quiet grace, a strength that didn't demand attention but commanded it nonetheless. Where girlfriends had brought thrill, she brought steadiness. Where others had filled moments with laughter, she filled life with meaning.

From the first morning after their wedding, he sensed the difference. The house smelt faintly of jasmine from the flowers she had arranged. Breakfast waited for him before work, and her smile—gentle, reassuring—made him want to come home each evening.

She stepped into his life with quiet authority, reorganising chaos into calm. Cushions that once slouched lazily on the sofa now stood neatly in place. His books, which he had sworn were in "creative order," now stood in tidy stacks. Even the flat itself seemed to breathe differently, scented with spices and warmth. The echo of temporary romances gave way to a home that felt permanent, steady, and alive.

And in private, marriage didn't erase passion—it transformed it. Their love was no longer the hurried business of cinema halls or the nervous trembling of first encounters. It was slower, steadier, more consuming. There was trust now, and with it, a deeper intimacy.

He discovered a new kind of romance: the joy of morning tea shared before the city awoke, her head resting on his lap as he scanned the newspaper, her voice humming in the kitchen while he stood in the doorway pretending to "supervise."

"Are you going to help or just stare?" she teased once, waving a spoon at him.

"Supervising is a form of help," he replied solemnly, before ducking to avoid the spoon.

Nights, too, carried a different fire. Some were filled with laughter, playful banter, and soft kisses stolen between jokes. Others burned hotter—the urgency of desire rekindled, but now with the ease of belonging. Their intimacy was no longer about proving love but living it.

Self-realisation crept in during the smallest gestures: the way he caught himself kissing her forehead before leaving for work, or how he instinctively reached for her hand in crowded markets without caring who noticed. The boy who once kissed nervously by the Gomti river was gone. In his place stood a man who could look across the dinner table and see not just a lover, but a companion for life.

Marriage hadn't dimmed the fire—it had given it direction. The thrill of the chase was replaced by the joy of building together, and Samarth realised, with a mixture of wonder and humour, that the greatest romance of all was not fleeting but steadfast.

Love After Marriage

Marriage did not put out the fire—it changed its colour. What was once wild and hurried now burnt slower, brighter, steadier.

The boy who had once fumbled with trembling hands now tied his wife's bangles with easy confidence. The man who once lingered nervously under streetlamps now shared his nights under the soft glow of a bedside lamp, their whispers lingering long after the city fell quiet.

He learnt that romance could bloom in the ordinary: brushing shoulders while cooking together, tugging playfully at her dupatta as she passed him tea, collapsing into laughter over something as silly as burnt toast. Even silence with her was full, layered with comfort.

Sometimes he woke to find her hair spilling across the pillow, her hand resting lightly on his chest. He would kiss her forehead before slipping out of bed, a silent promise renewed each morning. Over breakfast, their conversations stretched from mundane grocery lists to dreams of a life they had yet to build.

Evenings carried their own rhythm. She waited with a lit lamp, a meal prepared, and a smile that melted the day's exhaustion. He returned weary from work, but when she teased him about his stubborn tie knot and tugged it loose, the weariness fell away. He pulled her close, wordless, because some emotions needed no language.

Nights belonged entirely to them. Sometimes playful, sometimes fiery, sometimes tender. But always assured, always whole. After passion came stillness—the comfort of entwined fingers, the rhythm of her breathing against his chest, the sense that, in this one room, the world was finally at peace.

With her, Samarth discovered that true intimacy was not about secrecy or conquest. It was about trust—the kind that allowed vulnerability and laughter, playfulness and passion, to exist side by side.

Marriage had given him more than a wife. It had given him a partner who steadied his ambition, a confidante who believed in his dreams, and a lover who turned ordinary nights into poetry.

For Samarth, love after marriage was not the end of romance—it was its truest beginning.

Reflection

Lucknow gave Samarth everything—his first pay cheque, his gleaming bike, his girlfriends, his wife, his daughter, and the foundation of his career. It was a city of contradictions, holding within it both passion and patience, freedom and responsibility, youth and the beginnings of maturity.

Looking back, Samarth often thought of it as a mirror. In its streets he had seen both the boy he was and the man he was becoming. The boy who once sped recklessly along leafy boulevards on his motorcycle found himself, years later, slowing down to carry his daughter carefully in his arms. The young man who once lived for cinema-hall kisses and hurried romances discovered that love, in its truest form, was quieter— folded into the daily rhythms of companionship.

In Lucknow, he learnt that love was not only in fiery kisses or whispered promises. It was in the small, ordinary acts of devotion: a woman ironing his shirt before a meeting, stirring cumin in a pan while humming under her breath, slipping her hand into his in a dark theatre, or waiting at night with a cup of tea when his day had drained him dry. Love was not just about being wanted; it was about being cared for.

And yet, Lucknow also carried its silences. Samarth remembered evenings when he stood on his balcony watching the sky bleed into orange and violet, the silhouettes of birds returning home. A loneliness pressed on him then—the ache of knowing that even in a city full of life, one could feel utterly alone. The smell of a neighbour's cooking wafted across the courtyard, making him long for Ranchi, for his mother's kitchen, for the careless laughter of siblings. Those moments taught him that freedom often came wrapped in solitude, and that growing up meant learning to live with both.

By the time he left, Samarth was no longer just a boy chasing freedom. He was a man—shaped by passion, steadied by devotion, and quietly prepared for a future where purpose and tenderness could walk side by side. Lucknow had tested him, tempted him, broken and remade him. It gave him roots even as it gave him wings. And when he looked back, he realised: the city had not only given him love, but had also taught him how to hold on to it without losing himself.

He carried Lucknow within him like an unseen compass, its contradictions etched into his choices, its lessons folded into his silences.

When work pulled him to other cities, he found himself comparing their hurried skylines to the measured pace of Hazratganj, their glass towers to the fading grandeur of Chowk. Each place demanded something new, but Lucknow had already taught him how to give without losing his center. He remembered how the city had shaped his patience, how its evenings had whispered that not every hunger needed to be answered in haste. In boardrooms, in crowded trains, even in quiet apartments, he carried that balance of longing and restraint. It reminded him that freedom was not running away, but standing still without fear. And in every gesture of love he offered, Lucknow's shadow lingered—quiet, enduring, the city that had raised him into himself again and again.

Chapter 4

Climbing the Ladder – Professional Success and Family Strength

Rising Above the Ordinary

Lucknow had transformed Samarth. The boy who once scraped through exams now carried himself with the quiet swagger of a man who knew his worth. Independence was no longer enough—he wanted to rise, to be remembered, to carve meaning into whatever he touched.

Publishing became his true classroom. Books gave him knowledge, yes, but it was people who gave him wisdom. He learnt how a principal's trust could open doors more valuable than contracts, how a bookseller's loyalty could anchor a whole district, how a teacher's recommendation could ripple through generations.

At a sales review, his manager remarked, "Samarth, you're not just selling books. You're selling belief." Samarth smiled, leaning back a little too comfortably in his chair. "Belief," he replied, "is the easiest thing to sell when you carry it yourself." The room chuckled, but one colleague later whispered half-joking, half-admiring: "Careful, Ranchi ka ladka… Delhi will make you arrogant."

And perhaps it did.

Lucknow's Gift, Delhi's Reward

Samarth's years in Lucknow had been more than just a career assignment—they had been a pilgrimage of self-discovery. What started as a hesitant transfer had turned into the very place where he had found his voice, built his courage, and proved to himself that he was capable of more than anyone, including him, had imagined. The applause of his colleagues, the respect of his seniors, and the quiet pride in his own heart—all wove together into a moment of recognition. When the company finally called him back to Delhi for a bigger role, it felt like life itself had whispered: *You are ready*.

The train that carried him back to the capital seemed symbolic. Each passing mile was a reminder of where he had started—an uncertain young man lost in the noise of Delhi—and where he was now: a leader, seasoned and steady. As the city skyline appeared, a flood of memories rushed in, but this time, they no longer carried the sting of insecurity. Instead, there was peace, the deep satisfaction of someone returning not in defeat, but in quiet triumph.

Delhi embraced him differently this time. The streets that once felt harsh now seemed like familiar allies. His office at the headquarter building was not just a space—it was a sign of arrival. Yet, the real victory awaited him at home, beyond titles and responsibilities.

Soon after his return, life gifted Samarth and Ruhi with a daughter. The first moment he held her in his arms became the defining scene of his journey. Her tiny hand clasped his finger, her fragile breath warmed his chest, and in that instant, every struggle, every long night of doubt, every scar he carried turned into a badge of honor. Fatherhood changed everything. The man who once fought only for survival now had a reason to build, to nurture, to dream beyond himself.

Each morning, as he left for the office, he paused by her cradle, his eyes lingering on her innocent smile. Her presence gave him strength greater than any promotion ever could. At work, his confidence was no longer driven by ambition alone—it was guided by the knowledge that every success created a future not just for himself, but for the little girl waiting at home.

Ruhi often teased him about the way he would rush back from meetings, eager to catch even a fleeting moment with his daughter before she drifted to sleep.

But Samarth didn't mind; in fact, those moments defined his days. Rocking her gently in his arms, humming lullabies he never knew he remembered, he felt more accomplished than in any boardroom.

Delhi, once a place of loneliness and unsteady beginnings, had become the stage of his greatest joy. He had returned as a professional with responsibilities, but more importantly, as a father whose heart beat in rhythm with his daughter's tiny breaths. For Samarth, climbing the ladder was not just about rising in career—it was about rising as a man, a husband, and now, a father.

And as life settled into this rhythm of office and home, another truth began to emerge—Delhi, with all its contrasts and contradictions, was not just rewarding him. It was sharpening him.

Delhi: The Sharpening

Delhi honed his edges. The city pulsed at a rhythm unlike anywhere else—its mornings alive with the chaos of metro rush, its evenings a chorus of chai-stained conversations at Connaught Place, its nights glowing neon with ambition that refused to sleep. Samarth absorbed it all greedily.

On Sundays, he wandered through the by-lanes of Darya Ganj where second-hand booksellers laid entire worlds on the pavement. He would kneel to flip through crumbling pages, half in awe, half amused, before rising and brushing the dust from his crisp shirt as though the bookseller's world and his own were leagues apart. Standing tall amid the stacks, he felt both small and limitless at once.

Delhi taught him contrasts—the art of closing deals over cappuccinos in Khan Market, yet finding equal joy in greasy parathas at a roadside dhaba. He could bow his head in reverence at a Gurudwara in the morning, then walk into a boardroom that same afternoon and command attention with the sharpness of his words. The city's style wasn't just in its clothes or its monuments—it was in its people, each carrying dreams larger than life. Samarth began to see himself as one of them.

At home, his daughter's laughter softened him; in the office, Delhi's relentless energy sharpened him. Together, they forged a balance he had never known before.

One evening, over drinks, a colleague slapped him on the back: "You're not Ranchi's boy anymore, Samarth. You're a Delhi man now." Samarth smirked, swirling his glass. "Ranchi built me," he said, "Lucknow polished me… but Delhi—Delhi taught me how to wear the suit."

The youngest son of Ranchi was slowly becoming a force—not only shaped by where he came from, but by the cities that moulded him. Lucknow gave him grace. Delhi gave him fire.

The Business of Sacrifice

With success came responsibility, but for Samarth it was not a burden—it was a creed. Family was his foundation, the ground from which every dream grew. Sacrifice, for him, was not loss; it was love transmuted into action.

When his elder brother faced setbacks, Samarth stepped forward without hesitation. He didn't weigh the cost. He didn't ask for thanks. He simply believed, almost stubbornly, that true strength was measured not in what you gain but in what you give.

"Why do you always rush in?" a friend asked once, exasperated.

Samarth shrugged, lighting a cigarette with deliberate calm. "Because if I don't, who will? A man who rises alone will one day fall alone. But a man who lifts others—he rises forever."

That philosophy bled into his work. Where others guarded their achievements, Samarth opened doors. Where peers clung to their comfort, he embraced sacrifice. Colleagues noticed the difference. "Your decisions," his manager once said, "have weight. Not because they're clever, but because they're human."

Slowly, the world began to see him differently. Friends admired how he balanced ambition with generosity. Family saw not just a brother or son, but a protector who turned his victories into theirs.

Sacrifice, for Samarth, became a kind of business—an economy of love where the returns were not measured in wealth, but in gratitude, unity, and respect.

The boy who once struggled to find his place had risen above the ordinary. Success had entered his bloodstream, sometimes making him proud, sometimes making him vain. But beneath it, sacrifice steadied him, anchoring the man he was becoming.

Family Dynamics

Relatives proudly introduced him at gatherings as "our successful brother." His name travelled warmly from one conversation to another, not as a tale of wealth or power, but as a story of resilience and sacrifice. His journey became proof that hard work, anchored in love, could transform lives. Every nod of admiration, every affectionate smile filled the room with gratitude—not just for Samarth's success, but for the bond it nurtured.

The younger generation grew up breathing this sense of togetherness. His brother, whenever speaking to his children, would gently remind them:

"Always remember—love is greater than anything. What he gives is not just support, but love. And love must always be respected and cherished."

The children listened wide-eyed. They learnt that success without sharing was hollow, that sacrifice was not weakness but strength, and that love was the truest inheritance a family could pass down. To Samarth, hearing those words was more than comfort—it was blessing. His life had become an example worth carrying forward.

Lucknow had given the family grace—lantern-lit evenings in courtyards, the aroma of kebabs drifting through the air, stories of his achievements told with reverence alongside tales of nawabs. Delhi, however, gave these bonds new rhythm. On Holi, the family spilled into colony lanes, laughter echoing above the chaos of colour. At Diwali, balcony lights twinkled against the sprawling skyline as the family gathered around the dining table—parathas, kachoris, and unspoken belonging uniting them. Sundays often meant wandering through Darya Ganj's book market, where Samarth, with a book in one hand and a child's palm in the other, reminded them that knowledge was the finest gift.

Festivals became more than rituals; they were

celebrations of unity. In weddings with the rhythm of dholaks, in cousins' cricket matches in Delhi's dusty parks, in the chaos and the banter—Samarth felt a richness no fortune could buy.

And yet, within that warmth, a quiet tension sometimes stirred. His wife, graceful and steady, wished for more of him at home. There were evenings when she looked at him across the dinner table, her smile kind but her voice firm:

"You belong to everyone, Samarth—to your colleagues, your principals, your family. But sometimes, I wonder if you still belong to me."

He sighed, rubbing his temples after a long day. "You know I'm doing this for us—for all of us. Can't you see?"

She nodded, but her silence lingered longer than the meal.

Career Highs

In the office, Samarth's world felt like another theatre altogether. The publishing house where he now worked hummed with urgency—its wooden desks scarred with decades of hurried notes, the faint smell of ink and paper forever in the air. His cabin bore the imprint of his rising stature: a heavy desk stacked with catalogues, a brass nameplate that gleamed in the light, a pinboard covered with maps, sales figures, and notes scribbled in his neat hand.

Colleagues often peeked in, some for advice, others just to watch him work. "Samarth, how do you always close the deal?" one young sales rep asked.

Samarth smiled, leaning back in his chair. "Simple. You don't sell books—you sell trust. Once they trust you, the books sell themselves."

It wasn't arrogance alone—it was belief. But sometimes the belief came wrapped in a sharp edge. In meetings, when seniors faltered over strategies, Samarth would interject with a crisp, "That won't work, sir. We need to think bigger." He was right often enough that even the sting of his words was forgiven.

The phone on his desk never stopped buzzing—principals seeking assurances, managers asking for targets, booksellers calling with thanks. He thrived on it, yet the pace wore him down. At home, the buzzing didn't stop. His wife frowned at the phone that interrupted dinners.

"Can you switch it off for just one evening?" she asked once, voice soft but heavy.

Samarth slipped the phone back into his pocket, guilty but defiant. "If I switch it off, someone else will answer. And then I'll lose what I've built."

Her silence cut deeper than her words.

Still, his reputation soared. He became the man trusted with impossible deals, the one who walked into boardrooms with calm assurance and walked out having turned doubt into belief. His calendar filled with invitations, his name carried weight, his presence commanded respect.

Yet even amidst global offers—Singapore, Dubai, London—his compass pointed home. One evening, a London offer letter rested in his hands. At Delhi airport, staring at the departure gate, he felt the tug of another life: sleek offices, global acclaim, easier climbs. But then his mind wandered back to Darya Ganj's dusty Sunday lanes, to the principals who counted on him, to children who opened books as though opening worlds. He tore the ticket into two, dropped it in a bin, and walked out into the buzzing Delhi night, strangely lighter.

It wasn't hesitation—it was conviction. For Samarth, contribution meant more than escape. Success wasn't measured by the cities he could conquer, but by the lives he could touch.

And yet, success carried its price: the distance his wife sometimes felt, the time his daughter missed, the weariness he concealed behind confident smiles. His career highs were dazzling, but the shadows of sacrifice crept into his home, demanding a reckoning he could not always postpone.

Two Identities, One Heart

By his early thirties, Samarth carried two identities with equal pride—identities that often clash in others, but in him found perfect harmony.

In the corporate world, he was Mr. Samarth—admired, respected, sought after. Principals knew him as the man who never broke trust. Booksellers saw him as a partner who valued loyalty more than profit. Managers found in him a professional who chased not just targets but meaning. His name carried weight, but it was not fear that commanded respect—it was faith.

Yet at home, the titles melted away.

He was the younger brother who still touched his elder's feet whenever he visited Ranchi, bowing low while his brother teased, "Ab toh bade aadmi ho gaye ho (You've become a big man now)." Samarth would smile, "Bade aadmi sirf baahar, bhaiya. Yahan toh main ab bhi chhota hi hoon (Big man only outside, brother. Here, I'm still the youngest)."

He was the father who could leave a boardroom full of charts and contracts to sit in a school auditorium just in time to see his daughter on stage. One afternoon, in Delhi, it happened exactly so. At 3:20 pm, managers were talking about closing an important deal. By 3:55 pm, Samarth was in a crowded school hall, dust motes dancing in the sunlight, clapping until Misha spotted him. Her face lit up, her nervousness melted, and in that smile he found more meaning than in any contract.

Later, walking home with her, she whispered, "Papa, you left office for me?"

"For you," he replied, his voice catching for reasons she could not yet understand.

For in her small hand curled in his, Samarth sometimes felt the echo of another hand—his mother's, guiding him to school on misty Ranchi mornings. He would remember the way she tucked his collar, her fingers smelling faintly of mustard oil, and the way his father's shadow loomed quietly at the doorway, pipe smoke curling into the evening air.

Watching Misha sketch at the table or fall asleep with a book across her chest, he often thought, If only Ma could see this. If only Baba could hear her laugh.

The ache of absence came in quiet waves. During Diwali, as he lit lamps on the balcony with his daughter tugging at his kurta—"Papa, higher, touch the stars!"—he remembered the glow of lanterns in Ranchi, his mother humming softly as she placed diyas along the courtyard walls. At Holi, when colours smeared across his cheeks and laughter filled the Delhi air, he missed his father's stern but amused voice warning, "Bas karo, warna sardi lag jaayegi (Enough now, or you'll catch a cold)."

He carried that longing silently, never speaking of

it, but always feeling it. His parents were gone, yet their presence lingered in the way he raised his daughter—with the same quiet love, the same unspoken strength.

Ranchi had given him his roots—the humility of small lanes and the warmth of parental care. Lucknow had added refinement, grace, and rhythm to his life. Delhi had sharpened him, taught him how to stand tall amidst chaos.

And as he stood between these cities, watching Misha grow, he realised he was now playing both roles—father and mother, protector and guide. He missed his parents deeply, but in every bedtime story he told her, in every braid he clumsily attempted when her mother was away, in every clap that echoed across her school hall, he honoured them.

By his early thirties, Samarth had become something rare—a man who could inspire applause in a boardroom at noon and laughter in a living room by dusk. A man who could miss his parents and yet give everything to his child, turning grief into love, absence into presence.

Not two lives, but one life lived deeply—two identities bound by a single heart.

Professional Sharpness

Samarth's career was never a matter of chance—it was

crafted, like stone chiselled into form. Every step was deliberate, every move measured. He leapt, but never blindly. He fought, but always with foresight.

When given charge of a new region, he didn't bury himself in sales charts alone. He boarded rickety buses, trudged dusty village roads, and sat in staffrooms listening to teachers air their frustrations over cups of sweetened tea. He asked principals not only what they lacked, but what they dreamed of. In one district, he realised glossy brochures meant nothing—trust lived in the voices of local teachers. So he organised workshops, not with fanfare, but with sincerity. Within months, books that had gathered dust on storeroom shelves became the staple of classrooms.

Rivals scoffed at first. Later, they studied his methods.

But success had a price. In office meetings, colleagues muttered that Samarth's rise was too fast, his influence too wide. Once, in a Delhi conference room thick with cigarette smoke and stale tea, a senior colleague snapped:

"You make it look easy, Samarth. But let's not forget, this is business, not a charity trust."

Samarth, leaning back in his chair, replied evenly, "Business dies without trust. Build the people, the numbers will follow."

The room was divided. Some nodded in quiet

agreement; others rolled their eyes. But Samarth had spoken not to please, but to be understood.

The Office Atmosphere

The office itself became an arena. Grey metal cupboards lined the walls, dusty fans whirred overhead, and posters of smiling children holding books decorated the dull corridors. Colleagues gathered around in groups—some genuinely curious about his approach, others waiting for him to stumble.

At lunch breaks, debates broke out.

"You waste too much time listening to teachers," one colleague sneered.

"And you waste too much time gossiping," Samarth shot back, half-smiling, but with steel in his voice.

Animosity lingered, not out of malice alone, but envy. His desk often drew juniors like a magnet—seeking advice, approval, or just encouragement. That warmth, which earned him loyalty, also bred resentment among those who led with fear.

Strain at Home

But while his public life soared, home sometimes bore the brunt. His wife, gentle yet sharp, carried silence like a blade.

One evening, Samarth returned late again. The

table was cleared, the house quiet except for the ticking of the wall clock. His daughter's notebook lay open on the sofa, her half-written poem waiting like an unfinished thought.

"She wanted you to hear it," his wife said softly, her back to him as she folded clothes.

"I'll listen tomorrow," Samarth muttered, loosening his tie. "Work ran late."

She turned, her eyes steady, voice calm but edged:

"Tomorrow? Samarth, do you know how many tomorrows she has already waited? She doesn't need your money. She needs your ears. She needs her father."

The words pierced sharper than any rival's sneer. Samarth sat down heavily, guilt pooling in his chest. He stared at the half-finished poem and whispered to himself, What use is applause outside if I cannot clap for her inside this home?

It was in such moments that doubt stirred, and with it, the faint beginnings of a spiritual search. Late at night, when the city outside roared with honking buses and barking dogs, Samarth sometimes sat by the window, watching the lone bird cutting across the dark sky. What is all this for? he wondered. Numbers rise, respect grows, but does it fill the silence I carry?

The Bhagavad Gita on his shelf—gifted long ago by a professor—began to call to him. He opened it one evening, not with devotion, but with curiosity. The verse he read spoke of selfless action, of doing without attachment to reward. For the first time, Samarth felt the lines speaking not as philosophy, but as instruction. He underlined the words, closed the book, and carried them quietly into his work.

Respect at Every Step

Respect became his shadow—not demanded, but earned, one interaction at a time.

At national seminars, while others drowned audiences in numbers and pie charts, Samarth told stories. Stories of classrooms where children's faces lit up at new books, of a teacher in a forgotten town who found her confidence again through better resources. Applause came not just for his eloquence, but because he reminded the industry of its purpose.

In offices, respect spoke in quieter ways. Juniors sought his advice, seniors sought his strategy. Once, when a new recruit botched a major pitch, colleagues whispered that the boy's career was finished. Samarth stepped forward, took the blame in front of management, then spent evenings training the recruit. Months later, that recruit became a top performer—his loyalty to Samarth unshakeable.

Even rivals acknowledged his weight. A competitor

once quipped at a Delhi book fair, "We don't fight your company, Samarth. We fight you." The comment was meant half in jest, half in admiration—but it rang true.

And yet, even amidst success, Samarth knew he was walking a knife's edge. Ego beckoned, frustration tugged at home, admiration tempted him into pride. But somewhere, in those verses he had begun to read at night, a balance stirred.

"Do the work," the Gita whispered, "but do not be owned by it."

Samarth was still learning that lesson—but he had already taken the first step.

Reflection

By the close of this threshold, Samarth stood tall—professionally sharp, personally fulfilled, and slowly, almost imperceptibly, turning inward.

The world saw the polished exterior: the man in crisp shirts, respected in boardrooms, admired in family gatherings. But within him, something quieter and deeper had begun to stir. Late nights, after the applause of meetings had faded and the household had fallen into sleep, Samarth sat by the window with an open book—the Bhagavad Gita, Tagore's verses, sometimes a worn notebook of his own reflections.

At first, it was curiosity. Then, it became discipline. And finally, it became an anchor. The restlessness that had once driven him from Ranchi to Delhi, from Delhi to Lucknow, was giving way to an inner stillness. He was learning that the true ladder was not only the one built in offices, but the one that rose inside the heart—step by step, towards peace.

His sacrifices no longer felt like losses; they were blessings that chiselled him. His loyalty was not obligation; it was devotion that flowed naturally, without calculation. His love was no longer the fever of youth, but a flame steady enough to warm everyone who came close.

He lived now by a principle that had grown unyielding within him: "Success means little unless it lifts others along with you."

And with this principle, Samarth was becoming something greater than a professional sCousinuccess. He was a man carrying two worlds—the world of action and the world of spirit—in quiet harmony. To his family, he was not only support, but proof that love, when lived as practice, becomes legacy. To himself, he was no longer merely the youngest son who had once stumbled, but a soul walking steadily toward a truth deeper than ambition.

It was this truth that made him not just a man of his time, but a treasure for his family, a legacy already in the making.

Bottom of Form

Chapter 5

Betrayals, Bonds, and the Shattering Loss

A House Built on Hope

On its best days, the house carried the soundscape of childhood—Misha and her cousins, Parth and Ayush, tumbling through the rooms like siblings born of the same parents. hey bickered like twins over the last piece of toffee, Ayush laughed so loudly the spoons in the steel tumbler rattled, and all three clamoured for Samarth the moment his shadow darkened the doorway.

Samarth had sworn a private oath: no matter how ruthless the office hours, the evenings would belong to the children. He lived for their ordinariness—Misha's crayon-bright drawings scattered across the sofa, Ayush's cricket scores scribbled on scraps of paper, Ayush's half-solved physics problems abandoned on the dining table like unfinished puzzles waiting for him.

Though Parth and Ayush were technically his elder brother's sons, Samarth never thought of them as nephews. He folded them into his heart as his own. Together, the three formed a protective pack—conspiratorial in whispers, mischievous in laughter, and fierce in loyalty.

There were nights when the house echoed with the thud of cricket balls ricocheting off the courtyard walls until neighbours shouted, "Bas, bas, raat ho gayi!" There were Sunday mornings when Misha staged little plays with her cousins as actors, draping old dupattas for costumes while Samarth sat cross-legged as their most devoted audience. Once, after a particularly chaotic skit, he clapped so loudly that Misha declared, "Papa, you clap louder than the whole mohalla!"

Moments of intimacy came too. When Ayush pressed his cheek to Samarth's shoulder and whispered, *"Chachu, kabhi kabhi darr lagta hai—sometimes I get scared,"* Samarth tightened his embrace and answered, *"Fear is just a gate. Walk through it, and you'll meet yourself on the other side."* And when Ayush sulked after a cricket defeat, Samarth took him for a ride on his bike through Delhi's glowing night streets, the warm wind loosening the boy's silence until he finally laughed again.

To Samarth, this was the true shape of family—not

defined by signatures or surnames, but by the stubborn persistence of love. Love chosen, love practised, love that held.

The Doctrine of Use

Ronit, Samarth's sister's son, is the eldest of the cousins and is now working at a renowned Fortune 100 company in the USA, carried himself with a quiet maturity that steadied the younger three. Where Misha's imagination spilled across pages, where Ayush's energy burst into cricket scores, and where Parth wrestled stubbornly with numbers, Ronit anchored them with calm encouragement. He wasn't loud, but his presence was grounding—as though he had inherited early the family's belief that strength lies not in noise, but in example.

In Samarth's home, use was never about exploiting others. It meant living with intent: using words to heal, using strength to uplift, using blessings to build harmony.

Around the dinner table, as lantern-light softened their faces, Samarth's parents often shaped the evening with their gentle voices. His father, with the authority of experience, would murmur, "Never forget the hands that help you. Gratitude is the root of every lasting bond." His mother, ladling daal into bowls, would add softly, "And remember—kindness must be practised, not just promised." These words were not commandments; they were melodies, stitched into the fabric of life.

The children absorbed them almost unconsciously. Gratitude was learnt in the passing of sweets during Diwali, in the respectful silence when elders spoke, in the laughter rising from shared meals. Kindness became second nature, a reflex as natural as breathing.

Ronit carried the lessons most visibly. His voice had a sincerity that made the younger ones pause, his gestures brought reassurance, his steady nature gave the others someone to lean on. Misha often looked to him when her confidence wavered, Ayush mimicked his calm in moments of defeat, and even Parth, stubborn as he was, softened when Ronit placed a hand on his shoulder.

Samarth would often pause at the doorway, watching them: Misha scribbling homework while Ayush acted out cricket scores, Parth bent stubbornly over his sums, Ronit guiding them with patience. His father, watching alongside him once, whispered with pride, "They are learning what truly matters." His mother, smiling as she set down a plate of fruit, said, "Values must be lived in front of them, not preached. See? They are watching us, more than they listen."

And Samarth knew she was right.

He believed these children were being raised in an atmosphere that would shape them for life—where use meant not using people for gain, but using values for connection.

He clung to this hope like a prayer: that gratitude, once planted in young hearts, would grow into a compass through every storm, guiding them not only toward success but toward bonds that endure. He trusted that while wealth might fade and triumphs may be forgotten, love practised daily would outlast them all—like the lingering fragrance of incense long after the lamp has gone out.

A Wedding Across the Sea

When news of a family wedding abroad reached their home, excitement rippled through the walls like music. It was Samarth's eldest brother's son who was getting married, and the thought of a destination wedding across the sea filled the family with both thrill and nostalgia.

Misha immediately began sketching dresses on scraps of paper—swirls of fabric and imagined jewellery. Ayush, wide-eyed, couldn't stop talking about the airplane ride, his arms stretched out like wings as he zoomed through the living room. Parth, ever the thoughtful one, quietly began folding shirts into a small bag, as if the trip might begin any second. For the children, weddings were never just rituals. They were carnivals of laughter, reunions with cousins, stories retold by elders, and nights that ended only when eyelids refused to stay open.

Yet, as the date drew closer, reality tapped gently at their dreams. The children's exams fell in the same week, and it became clear that not everyone could travel. The thought of missing the wedding cast a shadow of disappointment over the house. But families, when bound by love, always find ways to bridge distances.

After long discussions, it was decided: the wedding would be live-streamed. Those who could not fly would join virtually, their laughter and blessings traveling across oceans through glowing screens. The elders agreed with a smile, reminding everyone that togetherness was not measured in miles, but in hearts that beat as one.

One evening, as Samarth sat polishing his shoes, Ayush tugged at his sleeve and asked softly, "*Chachu*, will we all go together?"

Samarth paused, looked into his nephew's searching eyes, and rested a hand on his shoulder. "Whether here or there, family is always together. Love doesn't need visas, beta."

Ayush thought quietly, his small fingers running over the edge of his passport. Then, with a gravity that startled the room, he slipped it back into the drawer. "This time, I'll stay home with you," he said gently, his voice carrying more maturity than his years.

The room fell into a tender silence. Misha reached out and hugged her brother tightly. "Then I'll make sure you don't miss anything," she declared, already sketching plans for decorations. Parth nodded, adding, "We'll all stay connected—no one is left behind." Samarth watched them, his heart swelling with pride. In their small gestures, he saw the strength of family—sacrifice, care, and togetherness.

That evening, instead of packing, the children transformed the house into a stage. Misha cut paper into garlands and taped them across doorways. Ayush beat out rhythms on an upturned steel plate, declaring himself the band. Parth, shy but smiling, joined in when Samarth clapped along. They played loud music on the tape recorder, twirled across the floor, and staged their own "wedding dance," complete with mock vows and bursts of laughter.

On the wedding day itself, the laptop and television became their window to the world across the sea. The bride's laughter rang out through the speakers, cousins waved from the other side of the globe, and the elders' blessings filled the room as though they were standing right there. Every few minutes, Ayush leaned closer to the screen, whispering greetings, clapping, and even doing a small dance so his cousins could see him. Misha proudly held up her homemade garlands to the camera, and Parth recited a blessing he had carefully written the night before.

The walls echoed as if they too were celebrating, the air thick with the smell of marigolds and the hum of joy. Across oceans from the actual wedding, in that small living room, they discovered a truth more radiant than ceremony: celebration was never bound by geography. It was bound, always, by love.

That night, when the children finally fell asleep, Samarth stood quietly by the window, the glow of the city lights washing over him. He thought of Ayush's small but powerful decision, of Misha's creativity, of Parth's calm steadiness, and of the family across the sea. A smile touched his lips. *The wedding gift was not just theirs to send, he thought. It was already here—in this home, in these bonds, in the love that kept us whole no matter the distance.*

The Call

It was an ordinary evening. The kitchen smelt of fresh tadka, cumin crackling in hot ghee, the familiar hiss rising as if life itself were breathing. Samarth was ladling steaming dal into a steel bowl, already thinking of calling Misha to the table. The ceiling fan hummed, utensils clinked, the children's chatter drifted from the next room—life in its simplest rhythm, unremarkable, unshaken.

Then the phone rang.

Not a lazy ring, not the unhurried trill of routine. This was sharp, insistent, splitting the air like an alarm bell in a dream. Samarth wiped his hand on a towel, picked up the receiver, pressed it to his ear.

The voice on the other end shattered like glass against stone. Words didn't form whole—they arrived in jagged shards: *"accident… drowning… hospital… hurry…"*

For a moment, Samarth couldn't place the sounds. They floated, meaningless, refusing to fit into sense. Then they pierced, and the bowl in his hand felt suddenly cold, emptied of heat. The kitchen shrank. The fan groaned louder, mocking his stillness.

His shoes refused to slip on. The road mocked him with red lights that refused to change, cars crawling as though time itself had conspired against him. Every turn elongated into a corridor without end. His heartbeat thundered inside his chest, as though it were trying to outrun the car.

And then—arrival.

White walls. The stench of antiseptic. A corridor alive with footsteps, whispers, the heavy air of dread. A nurse's face turned away, a doctor's words too measured to be merciful.

A sheet.

And beneath it, a boy's face too calm, too pale, too silent to belong to Ayush—the boy who once rattled spoons with laughter, who tore through afternoons with cricket bats and dust-streaked joy, who leaned into Samarth with questions too big for his age.

The earth didn't split—it tilted. The axis of the world shifted, and Samarth fell into a silence that was louder than screams. His throat closed. His chest burned. He tried to call Ayush's name, but the air wouldn't carry it.

One thought pounded, merciless, in his skull: *This cannot be my boy. Not Ayush. Not the laughter, not the mischief, not the spark. Not gone.*

But reality is a stone that does not yield. And reality said: he is gone.

Rituals without Oxygen

The rituals came like furniture dragged into a house—heavy, unwanted, impossible to move. Garlands sagged against walls. Incense smouldered into smoke that rose, curled, and died mid-air, carrying no solace. Cotton threads were tied, lamps flickered, mantras chanted, their syllables mechanical, echoing into the void where Ayush should have been listening.

Neighbours pressed trays of sweets into trembling hands, their voices repeating empty formulas: "Be strong… time heals… it was God's will." But in that house, time was no longer a river. It was a stone—immovable, suffocating.

Relatives wept and consoled, words falling like leaves on fire. Nothing took root. Nothing soothed. The house had lost its air.

In a corner, Misha clutched a cushion tight to her chest as if it were her brother's ribs she could still protect. Her voice cracked through the silence, thin as paper: "Papa… why did God take Ayush?"

Samarth bent over her, his lips trembling against her hair. His arms closed around her with desperation, as though he could hold back the tide of grief by sheer force. His voice, breaking, whispered: "Some questions even fathers cannot answer."

Across the room, Ayush's parents sat like hollowed-out statues. His father—usually a man of precise words and measured gestures—now rocked slightly, his hands knotted together, knuckles white as if he could squeeze sense out of the void. His mother swayed with low sobs, clutching the boy's school jersey against her chest, her hair dishevelled, her voice breaking into a keening that silenced even the priests. "My son… my son…" she whispered again and again, as if the repetition could drag him back from the water.

Samarth's elder brother turned his face toward the floor, unable to meet anyone's eyes. At intervals he rose abruptly, pacing the courtyard, fists clenched, muttering half-prayers, half-accusations: "Why him? Why my boy?" Then he would collapse back beside his wife, burying his face in his palms. His grief was not just tears—it was rage at the unfairness of life, at God, at himself for not being there.

That night, the house sank into darkness. Samarth walked into Ayush's room as though stepping into a shrine. The air smelt faintly of sweat and talc. On the desk lay an open book, corners worn, thumbprints pressed into the paper like fossils of presence. Against the wall leaned the cricket bat, scarred by victories in sunlit fields. On the shelf, folded neatly, a small receipt—for a gift Ayush had chosen, but never lived to give.

Every object screamed without sound. Foam remembered his weight, wood his touch, paper his patience. They stood loyal, bearing witness. But flesh, the one thing Samarth needed, had betrayed him—

gone, vanished into water's ruthless silence.

The room had become a tomb without stone, breathing without oxygen. Love still filled it, desperate and unspent, but the boy it clung to was no longer there.

And Samarth, standing in the dim light, realised grief was not an intruder. It was now a resident—settled, immovable, a shadow that would never leave the house.

Grief's Threshold

After the rituals, after the relatives had left carrying their whispers and platitudes, after the incense smoke had thinned to nothing, Samarth sat alone in Ayush's room. The cricket bat against the wall seemed to lean toward him, accusing and helpless all at once. The book on the desk remained open, a half-read sentence staring back like an unfinished life.

He touched the receipt Ayush had folded so neatly. His fingers trembled as though holding parchment sacred, as though this small paper carried more weight than gold.

For days, Samarth drifted between numbness and storm. At work, he signed contracts, smiled at principals, encouraged juniors—but his eyes betrayed a distance, a gaze fixed on something beyond charts and numbers. At home, he listened to Misha's questions, to Parth's sobbing silence, to Ronit's confused clapping as though it could restore joy. He tried to be anchor, but inside, he was adrift.

The First Turning

One night, when the house finally slept, Samarth wandered to the terrace. Delhi's sky stretched above, not full of stars but choked with haze, a few stubborn constellations flickering like embers through smoke. A lonely bird wheeled against the night, its cry sharp, unanswered.

Samarth closed his eyes. The city's noise softened until he heard only his breath, shallow and uneven. In that stillness, he whispered—not to God, not to any deity, but into the void: "Where are you, Ayush? What do I do with this emptiness?"

No answer came. Only the breeze, carrying with it the faint aroma of someone else's dinner—onions, ghee, and spices mingling with the night. Life went on in other kitchens. In his, silence had replaced hunger.

That silence became his teacher.

A Discipline of the Soul

Slowly, almost imperceptibly, Samarth's habits shifted. He still woke at dawn, but before newspapers and trains, he sat in quiet. No chants, no elaborate rituals—just breath, counted and observed. What began as an attempt to steady grief grew into a daily pilgrimage inward.

Colleagues noticed. Once, after a heated argument in the office, when tempers flared and accusations flew, Samarth simply listened. He did not retaliate, though the words thrown at him were sharp. Later, a colleague muttered, half in awe, half in jest: "Samarth, you sit there like a stone—you don't break, you don't even bend."

He smiled faintly, not to boast but because he understood: the stone was not hard, it was anchored. Pain had carved depth into him, and in that depth, he found a steadiness others mistook for strength.

At home, when Misha struggled with her grief, he no longer tried to explain away the loss. Instead, he sat beside her, wordless, letting her lean against his arm until the sobs quieted. Silence had become his form of prayer.

From Absence to Presence

In time, grief transfigured into something else—not lighter, not kinder, but deeper. Samarth began to see Ayush not in objects but in essences: the laughter of boys playing cricket in the colony, the impatient clatter of spoons at mealtime, the echo of footsteps racing up the stairs.

Ayush's absence became a presence, woven into the rhythm of Samarth's days. It was unbearable, but it was also unignorable. And so Samarth began to live as if every act—every meal, every word, every kindness—was an offering to the boy who could no longer do them.

The Solid Core

By then, Samarth's spiritual turn was not fragile or tentative. It was solid, unyielding, forged in fire. He no longer asked why. He accepted that some questions are beyond fathers, beyond men, beyond even priests.

Instead, he asked: What can I do with this pain?

And the answer that returned, again and again, was simple: turn it into love.

Love for Misha, whose childhood had lost its brother. Love for Parth, who wrestled with fears he could not name. Love for Ronit, toddling into a world that would need the light Ayush had once carried. Love for colleagues, juniors, strangers—anyone who crossed his path.

Samarth's spiritual streak was not cloistered in temples or scriptures. It was lived daily—in restraint when anger tempted him, in patience when frustration boiled, in generosity when selfishness beckoned.

And so, beneath the grief, he found a core no tragedy could shake. Solid, unyielding, quietly luminous.

The Empty Chair

At dinner, the geometry of the table was broken. Four plates, three mouths. One chair no one dared to remove, as if touching it would erase the last trace of Ayush. It stood there, stiff and accusing, a reminder that absence had weight.

His mother placed his plate there anyway, her hands trembling as she served dal onto it, as though he might return, late from a cricket match, sweaty and laughing. But the food sat untouched, steam fading into nothingness. Beside her, his father chewed without chewing, his jaw moving but no taste reaching him. Once a man of control, he now picked grains of rice with the absentmindedness of someone trying to hold back an ocean.

Misha lifted her spoon, then set it down again. Once, twice, three times, before forcing herself to eat. The clink of metal against the plate felt louder than usual, jarring in the stillness. Even the fan hummed differently, its rhythm fractured, as if the house itself knew something had shifted.

Samarth chewed with the care of dismantling a bomb, each bite deliberate, cautious, unnatural. Food no longer nourished; it was only a duty performed for survival. His wife kept her head bent low, as though prayer might be hiding inside the dal and rice. Silence stretched across the table like another guest no one had invited.

Once, Ayush's father tried to speak. His voice cracked mid-sentence. "He would have… he loved…" but the words refused to land. He stood abruptly, chair scraping the floor, and walked away. Moments later, muffled sobs seeped through the walls. His wife, clutching the end of her saree, whispered into the emptiness, "Who will call me Ma now with that laugh? Who will eat the last roti and fight with Misha over the smallest piece?"

The air was unbearable. They sat not to eat, but to endure, each breath heavier than the food before them.

Later, when the meal was over and the house pretended to sleep, Samarth retreated to the prayer room. The small space glowed faintly from the brass lamp, its flame wavering against the framed gods on the wall. Incense still smouldered from the evening ritual, but its fragrance now clung to the air like sorrow made visible.

He knelt, not with devotion but with collapse, his forehead pressing against folded hands that trembled. Around him, the silence was absolute—broken only by the faint crackle of the wick and the distant hum of ceiling fans from other rooms. The gods stared back in stillness, their eyes carved in wood and stone, offering no answers.

His tears fell soundlessly onto the floor, darkening the cool marble. They carried no wail, no cry, only the weight of a thousand unsaid words—the cricket matches he would never watch with Ayush, the laughter that would never rattle spoons again, the promise of a future that had been stolen by water's silence.

In that prayer room, beneath the indifferent gaze of deities and the wavering flame, Samarth wept the way men pray—quietly, debt-like, unseen. His grief rose like incense smoke, curling upward, seeking a heaven that gave no reply. And in that silence, he understood with brutal clarity: the boy who once filled his world would never again return to the empty chair.

The Letter He Never Sent

He sat at the desk, trembling fingers holding the pen as though it were too heavy for a single hand. Paper waited like a witness. And so, he wrote to the boy who could not answer:

> *Beta,*
>
> *I bought the notebook you wanted. It's still wrapped, lying untouched on the shelf, waiting for you to scribble your dreams across its pages. Your bat is in my cupboard—I couldn't bear to leave it leaning by the wall like it used to. Every time I open the door, it stares at me, asking why it no longer rests in your hands.*

Your teacher cried when he said your name. He called you a bright star, and I wanted to tell him—you still are. But the world has no language for light that burns without a body.

If you see us from where you are, look longer at Misha. She keeps smiling so I can survive. Her smile is stitched with courage, but I know it is threadbare. She whispers to your pillow, as if it might answer her in dreams. Watch her, son. Guard her the way I no longer can.

Sometimes I hear your mother calling you in her sleep. Sometimes I see your father's hands shaking when he lights the lamp, as though the flame itself knows what it has lost. Stay near them if you can, even in silence. They need you more than they can bear to admit.

The ink blurred as his eyes brimmed, his tears staining the very words he wanted his son to read. He pressed the paper to his chest, holding it there as though the beating of his heart might carry the message across some impossible distance.

Then, with hands that shook like leaves in a storm, he tore the letter into pieces no larger than breath. Each fragment fluttered down like broken wings, scattering across the floor, words meant for eternity reduced to silence.

And in that silence, a father's brother, a family's

uncle, a man shattered by love, realised this truth: grief has no grammar. It lingers in empty chairs, in broken voices, in the ache of letters never sent.

Home as Healing

Home became both refuge and repair. His wife did not drown him in words-she offered presence, steady and quiet, like the anchor of a ship in storm. She brewed his tea without asking if he wanted it, sat beside him in silence when words were too heavy, and sometimes just placed her hand on his arm, reminding him he was not alone.

Misha, still a child yet wise beyond her years, became his unexpected healer. She straightened his slippers near the door, left small sticky notes on his desk with doodles and words like *"Smile, Papa"* or *"You're my hero."* She tugged him into ludo games late at night, insisting on laughter, even if forced. Once, when he tried to refuse, she crossed her arms and said, *"If you don't play, Papa, Ayush will be sad."* He sat down, rolled the dice, and for the first time in weeks, the sound of laughter-thin but real-returned to the house.

Through these tiny rituals, the house learnt to breathe again. It did not erase the absence, but it filled the silence with threads of togetherness.

Choosing Boundaries

Grief had carved new shapes into Samarth's soul. Once, he believed love meant giving without end pouring himself out for anyone who asked, carrying burdens that were never his own. But Ayush's absence changed him. It did not harden him; it clarified him. He began to understand that love without balance could hollow a man, leaving nothing left for those who truly needed him.

The first time he said *"no"* to a family request, it felt like lifting a mountain with bare hands. His throat tightened, his palms sweated, his heart raced as though he were betraying some sacred duty. Yet when the words left his lips, he felt something unexpected: release. For the first time, he had drawn a fragile circle of protection around the part of himself still bleeding.

He sat alone afterward, guilt and relief warring in his chest. Then he looked at Misha, her small frame curled into his side, her hand clutching his as though he were her last anchor. He looked at his wife, who carried her grief like a second heartbeat, steady but unspoken. In their eyes, he saw the truth: if he scattered himself to the winds, what would be left for them?

It was not bitterness. It was clarity. To honour Ayush was not to break himself in endless sacrifice, but to gather strength for the living who leaned on him. He began to see boundaries not as walls, but as shields-protecting the fire of love so it would not burn out.

Love, he discovered, was not a river that had to drown him. It was a well he could guard, draw from, and offer with intention. Saying *no* became a way of saying *yes* to what mattered most: to Misha's laughter slowly returning, to his wife's quiet resilience, to the memory of Ayush who deserved to be remembered with light, not exhaustion.

And so, grief taught him something unexpected. That love endures not because it has no limits, but because it learns when to rest, when to preserve, and when to protect its flame. Boundaries, he realised, were not the end of love, but the form that kept it alive.

The Day After the Worst Day

When Ayush's 20th birthday arrived, the air in the house was heavier than any silence Samarth had known. The date itself seemed cruel, etched on calendars, circled in memories, but emptied of the boy it belonged to. The absence felt sharper, more merciless, as if the world were reminding them of what they had lost.

Yet Samarth could not let the day pass like any other. He rose early, walked into Ayush's room, and sat quietly on the edge of his bed. The sheets still carried faint creases, the desk still held the echoes of his son's laughter. He placed a small chocolate bar-the kind

Ayush always asked for-on the desk. Leaning closer, his voice trembled in a whisper only the walls could hear: *"Happy birthday, beta."*

All day, the house moved gently, cautiously, as though afraid to break under the weight of memory. No balloons, no songs, no noise, just a fragile kind of reverence. When evening came, Misha entered the dining room carrying the chocolate. Her hands were steady, though her eyes glistened. She broke it carefully into small pieces, like it was something sacred. Then she held one piece out to her father.

"For Ayush," she said firmly, her voice braver than her years.

Samarth froze. His chest ached with the collision of pride and sorrow. His hand shook as he reached out, accepting the offering. He placed it in his mouth, and as the chocolate melted, sweetness mixed with the salt of his tears. It was the most painful, beautiful bite he had ever taken.

The house did not erupt in celebration, but it did not remain hollow either. No laughter filled the air, yet neither did despair claim the night. Instead, in that simple act of remembering-of sharing a small chocolate, grief was reshaped into ritual.

It became proof that love does not end with death. That even after the worst day, love finds a way to return to the table, to sit quietly among the living, to bind them together in both ache and tenderness. Ayush was gone, but he was still there-present in sweetness, in memory, in the courage of a sister and the tears of a uncle who refused to let his boy's birthday vanish into silence.

The New Promise

There came a day when Samarth realised he could no longer be everything for everyone. Before, a single phone call was enough-he would rush, wallet open, shoulders ready to bear any weight. But grief had carved him raw, and in that emptiness he found clarity.

He began to count his "yeses" carefully. Each one now carried meaning. He was still generous, but no longer boundless. He gave, but not at the cost of his own wounds. He offered presence, but not his entire soul.

When distant relatives called only in times of need, he paused before answering. When colleagues asked for favours that drained him, he smiled, but declined. And when Misha tugged at his sleeve, whispering, *"Papa, let's talk,"* his yes was immediate, wholehearted.

This was his new promise: his love would remain fierce, but it would no longer be purchasable. He would live for the people who truly lived with him.

And in making that promise, a quiet strength rose inside him-the strength of a man who had given everything once, and now knew the sacredness of holding some part of himself back, for himself, for his daughter, for Ayush's memory.

What Remains

Grief leaves behind objects heavier than mountains. An empty chair at the dining table. A cricket bat with faded scuffs from a hundred matches. A receipt for a gift Ayush had never given, tucked in a book that still smelt faintly of ink and youth.

Each item was ordinary once. Now, each carried unbearable weight. Samarth could not pass by without his chest tightening, without tears stinging his eyes. Sometimes he reached out and touched the bat, tracing the handle as though it might still be warm from Ayush's hands. Sometimes he opened a drawer and found a folded shirt, its collar creased, and sat holding it for long minutes, the fabric wet with silent tears.

But grief, in its cruel teaching, also revealed courage. It taught him to say no without guilt, to give without erasing himself, to live with sorrow as a companion instead of an enemy.

Sorrow stayed-it always would. Yet within that sorrow was a new kind of steel, wrapped in the silk of love. It was not hardness, but resilience. Not denial, but acceptance.

What remained was this: a father's vow to honour both the boy who was gone and the girl who remained. To let Ayush's laughter live on in memory, and to make Misha's laughter echo louder in their home. To carry loss in one hand and love in the other-and to walk forward, not as a man unbroken, but as a man remade.

Reflection: The End of Innocence, the Beginning of Wisdom

Ayush's death did not end love. It tore it apart, scattered it into pieces, and then forced Samarth to gather those pieces back together in a new shape. The love that returned was not naïve-it was raw, scarred, and eternal.

He still loved fiercely-Misha, whose quiet strength saved him more than once; Ayush, whose youthful energy carried reminders of play; the children he mentored at work, who unknowingly received the tenderness he once poured into Ayush. But now he understood: love was not blind surrender. Love needed wisdom, boundaries, and truth.

He also learnt a truth that cut deep-masks exist even at funerals. Sometimes people cry without feeling, speak without meaning. And so he discovered that *true family* is not always written in the surname you share, but in the ones who laugh at your dining table, who sit beside you in silence, who weep with you without asking for anything in return.

Storms, he realised, are not survived by being harder than them. They are survived by being truer.

Family Traditions Renewed

The pain of Ayush's absence was unbearable, yet the family chose not to let it silence them. On birthdays, they placed an extra chocolate on the table. On Diwali, they lit one extra lamp. On every festival, one small ritual belonged solely to Ayush-*"for him,"* they would say.

The gestures were simple, but they were lifelines. They reminded the house that love does not vanish with death; it continues, reshaped in memory.

One evening, after placing a slice of cake in front of Ayush's photo, Misha whispered, *"Papa, it feels like he is still with us."* Samarth's throat tightened, tears burning, but he managed a nod. *"Yes, beta. He is."*

In that moment, Samarth realised that remembrance was not about graves or garlands. It was about laughter carried forward, lessons retold, kindness extended in his name. Ayush breathed not only in photographs, but in actions, in rituals, in the lives he continued to inspire.

The Wisdom of Loss

Ayush's absence was a wound that would never fully close, but within that wound bloomed a new depth. Samarth discovered that love is not erased by death-it is reshaped into something quieter, stronger, and strangely more enduring.

He learnt that grief, when carried with grace, becomes strength. That rituals, when filled with sincerity, can heal more than they hurt. And that true remembrance is not only in mourning, but in living fully-continuing the laughter, the learning, and the light of the one lost.

The innocence of believing that life would always give was gone. But in its place came wisdom-the wisdom to cherish moments as they happen, to say "I love you" without delay, to treasure the people who truly matter.

And so, through pain, Samarth emerged not broken, but remade. He carried sorrow in one hand, love in the other, and walked forward with the resolve that Ayush's light would never fade-because it now burned inside him.

Chapter 6

Rebuilding Through Work – Turning Pain Into Power

The Fire After the Storm

When Ayush died, it felt as if the world itself had collapsed. Walls that once echoed with laughter stood hollow, and evenings once filled with chatter now hummed with silence. Yet in that silence, something stirred inside Samarth-a fire that refused to go out.

Grief has two faces. For some, it consumes. For others, it reshapes. For Samarth, it became transformation. Where there had once been despair, there now glowed an unyielding determination.

He could not change fate. He could not bring Ayush back. He could not undo the questions that haunted him- *"What if we had gone? What if I had done more?"* But there was one thing he could command with certainty: his work.

It became his rebellion. *If death could strike without warning, then the only true answer was to live with purpose.*

Work as a Weapon

Samarth began to see his office desk as a battleground. Spreadsheets, presentations, and sales targets were no longer just professional tasks-they were shields and swords.

When colleagues wondered why he was suddenly the first to arrive and the last to leave, they mistook it for ambition. It was survival. The rhythm of typing, the structure of meetings, the clarity of deadlines gave him something grief could not-control.

Case Study: Once, while presenting to a room of principals, he found himself speaking about *"the responsibility of teachers to plant seeds that outlive us."* His words were meant for education, but every sentence carried Ayush in it. One principal later told him, *"Samarth ji, you don't just sell books, you remind us why we teach."* That day, Samarth realised his pain had found a voice through his work.

Purpose Beyond Numbers

Targets were met, deals were signed, but for Samarth the real victory was different. Each book sold, each school convinced, each child holding a new textbook was, in his mind, a tribute.

He began to imagine Ayush in every child. When he saw a boy hunched over a notebook, he thought of

Ayush's unfinished physics problems. When he passed a playground full of laughter, he thought of Ayush's cricket bat, still leaning in his room.

So when he worked, it was no longer for salary slips or performance reviews. It was to ensure that somewhere, in some classroom, a child's laughter and learning would continue where Ayush's had stopped.

The Fuel of Pain

Grief did not weaken him-it sharpened him. Competitors noticed his relentless focus. Managers admired his resilience. But what they did not see were the nights he wept quietly, only to rise at dawn determined to build something meaningful.

Example: Once, after a gruelling week of travel, he returned home late at night. Misha, waiting up with a small drawing in her hand, said, *"Papa, this is you with a fire inside."* The sketch showed a stick figure with flames in its chest. Samarth stared at it for a long time, realising his daughter had captured what words could not.

The Office as Sanctuary

The office became more than a workplace – it became his sanctuary, his temple. Each morning, while others groaned at alarms and dragged their feet to work,

Samarth rose early, ironed his shirt with precision, polished his shoes until they gleamed, and walked into the office as though stepping onto sacred ground.

His desk was not just a desk. It was a battlefield. The files stacked on one side were like shields, the reports like ammunition, the targets pinned to the wall like enemy flags to be conquered. Every phone call answered, every contract negotiated, every line of a proposal written was a blow struck against despair.

He threw himself into sales pitches with unmatched energy. Where others rehearsed lines, he told stories. Where others sold books, he sold dreams. Once, in a crowded hall of school principals, he compared education to planting an orchard: *"One book in a child's hand is a seed. And seeds never stop at one tree. They grow into forests."* The room erupted in applause. For the principals, it was inspiration. For Samarth, it was catharsis-the sound of hands clapping was the sound of life pushing back against silence.

Nights stretched into mornings. Long after the office emptied, his lamp stayed on. He crafted strategies, reshaped campaigns, polished presentations until every slide glowed with clarity and conviction. He was no longer working for quarterly reports alone-he was sculpting himself anew, brick by brick, sentence by sentence, slide by slide.

His managers noticed the change. In review meetings, they spoke in hushed admiration: *"This man doesn't just deliver-he transforms."* His juniors looked up to him, not because he demanded respect, but because he embodied it. He stayed late to mentor them, coached them through their first failed pitches, and celebrated their smallest victories as if they were his own. Many whispered that working under Samarth was like being in a classroom where every mistake was forgiven but every lesson remembered.

Even competitors grudgingly acknowledged him. Rivals who once dismissed him as "just another sales executive" now found themselves studying his moves. One competitor admitted at a conference, *"We don't compete against his company-we compete against Samarth."*

What they did not know was that beneath the polished suit and sharp strategies lay a man still mourning. Every file he closed was a way to keep grief at bay. Every handshake sealed was a promise to himself: that sorrow would not swallow him.

He wasn't just working. He was rebuilding. Each contract signed was a brick laid. Each school convinced was a pillar raised. Each success story was mortar filling the cracks left by loss.

And slowly, the rubble of grief turned into the architecture of resilience.

Leadership Emerges

Grief had stripped away his casualness. The young man who once relied only on charm and instinct was now methodical, disciplined, relentless.

This transformation made him a natural leader. Juniors began seeking him out, not just for professional advice but for personal guidance. He became a mentor, teaching them not only how to sell but how to survive-in business, in family, in life.

"Sir," one of them said once, "you don't just talk about targets. You talk about living."

Samarth smiled, but inside, he thought: ***If only you knew the price of this wisdom.***

Offers He Refused

As his stature grew, the offers abroad returned. Companies in Dubai, Singapore, even London wanted him. The salaries were dazzling, the perks impossible to ignore.

But Samarth stayed firm. "No," he said each time. "I will build here."

It wasn't just patriotism. It was defiance. Why should he leave his soil when he could prove that success was possible here? Why should he escape when India was the place where his struggles, his triumphs, his losses, and his love all lived?

Home: Love and Healing

At home, the bond with his wife deepened. She had seen him broken after Ayush's death, and now she watched him rise again. She said little, but her eyes carried pride.

Their intimacy, once fiery in youth, had matured into something profound. Nights were no longer just about discussion but about healing. Their closeness was a way of saying: *We are still alive. We still belong to each other. The world has not defeated us.*

Misha, too, became a quiet force in his life. Her innocence, her laughter, her questions pulled him back whenever grief threatened to swallow him. She reminded him of what was still left, of what was worth fighting for.

Family Shadows

The family, however, did not change. The same opportunism, the same entitlement, the same unspoken expectation that Samarth would always be there, carrying weight without complaint.

But now, Samarth saw through it. He gave when necessary, but no longer blindly. He began setting boundaries. He smiled politely at manipulation but no longer fell for it.

This shift unsettled them. They called him distant,

cold. But Samarth had simply learnt the truth: family loyalty without limits is not love-it is slavery.

The Birth of a Vision

As his career stabilised, Samarth began to dream bigger. Why remain an employee, bound by the decisions of others, when he had the skills to lead?

Late at night, he scribbled notes in diaries-business ideas, models, potential partnerships. He thought of creating something of his own, not just for money but for legacy.

He imagined a company where employees were treated with respect, where education wasn't just business but impact, where loyalty was rewarded, not exploited. A company built not on greed but on values.

This vision grew inside him like a seed demanding soil.

Turning Grief Into Creation

Samarth often thought of Ayush when planning his future company. He imagined the boy working beside him, handling accounts, laughing in meetings, bringing youthful energy into the office. That vision hurt, but it also motivated.

"If he cannot live his dreams," Samarth told himself, "I will live mine-and his too."

This became his silent oath: to turn grief into creation, to turn loss into legacy.

Strength in Silence

What struck people most about Samarth in these years was his silence. He didn't boast, didn't seek attention. His success spoke for itself.

At family gatherings, he was polite but reserved. At work, he was respected but humble. He had no need to prove himself with words; his journey had already proven him with scars.

This silence carried power. It made people lean in when he finally did speak, because his words were never wasted.

Reflection

Samarth's present win was not about outward victories alone. It was about the invisible war inside him.

Grief had tried to crush him, family had tried to use him, fate had mocked him. And yet, he rose-not by denying his pain but by transforming it into power.

Samarth rebuilt himself through work, through love at home, through silent strength, and through the vision of creating something larger than himself.

He was no longer just the youngest son from

Ranchi. He was a man forged in fire, ready to build, ready to lead, ready to prove that even when life breaks you, you can rise stronger than before.

Chapter 7

The Birth of a Company – Building Legacy from Pain

The Seed of an Idea

By the time Samarth entered this new phase of life, his name already carried weight across the publishing industry. Principals trusted him, teachers remembered him, and bookstore owners greeted him with warmth. Managers relied on his judgment, and even competitors spoke his name with respect. He had climbed to a place where most would have been content.

But Samarth was not made for contentment. Comfort, to him, was simply another word for stagnation. His heart still carried the heaviness of Ayush's absence, and his mind-restless, sharp, unyielding-refused to sit still.

He began to ask himself questions that refused to leave him alone:

- *Was success only about higher salaries and foreign postings?*
- *Couldn't a company be more than a business-a family, a mission, a living story?*
- *What if the scars of my journey became the foundation of something greater?*

These questions grew louder each night as he scribbled in his diary by the light of a table lamp. On those pages were not just words, but visions:

- *A company where employees were not workers but family-celebrated in both success and struggle.*
- *A company where education was not just a product to be sold, but a mission to spread knowledge, joy, and dignity.*
- *A company that would carry his name, his scars, and his dreams into the future-a legacy that even Ayush could be proud of.*

For years, these thoughts had remained quiet sketches at the back of his notebooks, ideas folded away like unplanted seeds. But now, something within him shifted.

Ayush's absence had taught him the brevity of life. And with that realisation came urgency. The seed no longer wanted to stay dormant.

It demanded soil.

Case Study: During a sales meeting, a principal once asked him half-jokingly, *"Samarth ji, why don't you start your own company? You don't just sell books, you sell trust."* Everyone in the room laughed. Samarth smiled too-but when he returned home that night, the words echoed in his ears. That laugh became a spark.

Case Study: A junior once told him, *"Sir, if one day you open your own publishing house, I'll be the first to join. Because you don't make us feel like employees-you make us feel like we matter."* Samarth didn't reply, but he wrote it down in his diary, underlined twice.

These moments, scattered like droplets, began to gather into a storm.

Samarth knew he was standing at a crossroads. On one side lay a comfortable career, promotions, and the safety of working for others. On the other lay uncertainty, sleepless nights, and the chance to build something extraordinary.

For most, the first road would be enough. But for Samarth, the second road was the only one worth walking.

The seed of an idea was no longer a dream. It was becoming a demand.

The Fear and the Fire

Starting a company was not a small decision-it was stepping off the edge of a cliff, unsure if wings would open or if the ground would break the fall.

Samarth knew the risks: financial, professional, personal. No more steady pay cheque, no cushion of a company's backing, no safety net of a title or brand. It meant replacing stability with uncertainty, and certainty with sleepless nights.

There were evenings when doubt crept in like an unwelcome guest. He would sit at the dining table, looking at his wife quietly serving food, at Misha sketching on the sofa, and wonder:

What if I fail?

What if this gamble takes away the very stability I've given them?

What if chasing my dream costs my family their peace?

His wife sensed his restlessness. Once, as he sat staring into his cold tea, she placed her hand over his and said, *"Whatever you decide, we'll stand with you. Don't fear failure-fear regret."*

Those words lit something inside him.

And then there was Ayush-always Ayush. Samarth remembered his laughter, his questions, his cricket bat leaning against the wall. He remembered how short life could be, how suddenly it could end.

If death could arrive without warning, then why live half-heartedly? Why stay safe when passion was calling?

The fear remained, yes-it never truly vanished. But fear was no longer an obstacle. It became fuel. Every heartbeat that once whispered *"what if you fail?"* now thundered *"what if you fly?"*

Samarth chose the fire.

He understood now: true risk was not in trying and failing. True risk was in never trying at all.

The First Step

Samarth typed his resignation letter with steady hands but a storming heart. The words were simple, polite, almost ordinary. But to him, it felt like breaking chains.

When he slid the envelope across his manager's desk, silence filled the room.

"Why leave when you are at the top?" his manager asked, eyes narrowing with disbelief.

Samarth's reply was quiet, but it carried the weight of destiny:

"Because the top here is still someone else's roof."

That one line hung in the air like a prophecy.

Within weeks, with nothing but his savings, an unshakable determination, and a vision larger than himself, Samarth registered his company. The name he chose wasn't flashy, but it was strong, grounded in purpose-like steel wrapped in silk.

When he held the certificate of incorporation in

his hands, it felt like cradling a newborn. Fragile, yes. Demanding, yes. But also alive with infinite possibility.

Building Brick by Brick

The early days were chaos disguised as progress. There was no plush office with glass walls or air-conditioned boardrooms. There was only a rented room with peeling paint, a rickety table, a borrowed chair, and a second-hand computer that whirred louder than an engine.

Samarth did everything. In the morning, he was the CEO-drawing up product plans, writing strategy notes on scraps of paper. By afternoon, he was the sales executive-knocking on school doors, pitching his vision to principals. By evening, he became the accountant-drafting invoices, balancing meager cash flows. And sometimes, at night, he swept the floor himself.

One day, after returning late from a school visit, he spilled tea on his only printed brochure batch. Instead of cursing his fate, he stayed up till dawn reprinting, stapling, and binding every copy himself. "If this is what it takes, I'll do it," he told himself.

Brick by brick, hour by hour, the dream began to take shape.

Slowly, he hired people-not just employees, but believers. Young men and women who didn't just work for salaries but for the fire they saw in Samarth's eyes. To them, he was not just a boss; he was a mentor. He trained them, stood by them, scolded when needed, but always reminded them: "We are not just building a company. We are building a family."

The one-room office grew into two, then into an entire floor, and finally into a building that bore the heartbeat of his dream.

The Family's Reaction

When word spread that Samarth had left a secure job to start his own company, reactions poured in. Some scoffed: *"Another experiment. Let's see how long this lasts."* Others smiled politely but whispered doubts behind closed doors.

Samarth didn't flinch. He had long stopped measuring his worth in borrowed validation.

Ironically, the same relatives who doubted him in private would later boast in public: *"He's our brother, our nephew, our son. Look what he has built."* But in those early days, when silence weighed heavier than support, Samarth learnt something invaluable-fuel burns hotter when ignited by doubt.

The Philosophy of the Company

From day one, Samarth insisted his company would be different. It would not just be another publishing house. It would be a philosophy, a mission, a living answer to his scars.

He treated employees with the respect he had once craved. He listened when they faltered, celebrated when they rose, and stood with them in storms. "We are not colleagues," he often said, "we are family. But the kind that lifts, not the kind that forgets."

His books were not just books. They were bridges-between teacher and student, between dream and destiny. Every page was designed with care, every illustration purposeful, every word crafted not to sell but to transform.

Customers noticed. Schools began to trust him. Principals called him back not just for books, but for advice. The reputation spread: this was not business. This was impact.

Success and Sacrifice

Success, however, never arrived without sacrifice.

There were months when payments were delayed and cash flow nearly strangled the dream. More than once, Samarth skipped his own salary to make sure his staff were paid on time. His wife quietly managed the household, never once complaining when expenses pinched. Misha grew up faster than most children, learning that her father wasn't just working-he was building.

Each sacrifice hurt, but each victory tasted sweeter.

The first big order.

The first profitable year.

The first time his company's name was spoken in a conference hall alongside giants of the industry.

Each milestone was carved out of sweat, sleepless nights, and stubborn resilience.

The Legacy in the Making

As years passed, Samarth's company transformed from a dream into a force. From small classrooms in Lucknow to the grand halls of metros, his books and ideas touched thousands of students.

And with each success, Samarth silently dedicated his victories. *This is for you, Ayush,* he whispered after every achievement. *Your dreams live here.*

Misha, too, grew into his proudest ambassador. When her friends asked what her father did, she smiled wide: *"My papa runs his own company."*

For Samarth, that was the truest reward-not the profits, not the fame, but the pride in his daughter's voice.

Reflection

This was not only the story of entrepreneurship. It was the story of resurrection.

Samarth had fallen, been bruised, and scarred—but he refused to remain in the dust. He turned grief into fuel, betrayal into a shield, scars into armour.

The company was never just a ledger of profits. It was his rebellion against fate, his cathedral built from ruins, his proof that wounds could be shaped into wings.

From Ranchi's scolded boy who once failed his exams rose a man whose name was engraved into the very pillars of an enterprise. A legacy carved not from privilege, but from persistence; not from comfort, but from the fire of endurance.

Samarth had not merely built a business. He had built a life that would stand taller than him, a life designed to outlive him.

Chapter 8

Trials of an Entrepreneur – Battles, Betrayals, and Breakthroughs

The Weight of a Dream

Dreams are heavy. No one tells you this when you begin. They only show you the shining side-the success stories, the smiling photographs of entrepreneurs standing with trophies and teams. They don't show you the weight-the endless nights when you sit in a dimly lit room, staring at the ceiling, wondering if the roof above your head might give way before your hopes take flight.

Samarth had chosen this weight. He had walked away from the comfort of a high-paying job, left behind the applause of stability, and stepped into the storm of uncertainty. With nothing but grit in his veins and grief in his heart, he set out to build a company. From the outside, it looked brave, even heroic. But from the inside, it often felt like madness-like dragging a mountain uphill with his bare hands.

Every day began before sunrise. He wore clean shirts, polished shoes, and carried a smile that convinced the world he was unbreakable. But the mirror knew the truth. When he looked into it each morning, he saw not just a man in pressed clothes but a warrior stitched with shadows-shadows of sleepless nights, unspoken fears, and questions no one could answer.

Will I survive another day?

Will this company live, or will it collapse with me?

The truth is, dreams don't float. They press down on your shoulders like a boulder. They demand more than strength-they demand sacrifice. They strip away illusions and test the steel of your spirit.

Samarth carried not only the weight of his company, but the weight of love and loss. The memory of Ayush haunted him-his laughter silenced too soon. That scar became a vow: every book printed, every child reached, every employee nurtured would whisper, *"This is for you, Ayush."* The grief that could have broken him instead became the foundation of his resolve.

At home, another dream waited-Misha. She was not just his daughter; she was his reason to endure. He bore the weight of her future on his shoulders too: sacrificing promotions, delaying comforts, saving every rupee for her education. Each decision in business was tied to a decision in fatherhood. Every time he wanted to give up, he looked at her eyes and remembered: *dreams are not carried for ourselves alone; sometimes, we carry them for those who cannot yet carry their own.*

And so, he pressed on. Through betrayals, through financial storms, through nights where silence screamed louder than applause. His company was never just a business. It was a mirror of his courage, a monument to resilience, and a message to the world:

- That success is not measured by profits, but by persistence.
- That scars are not shame-they are survival's signature.
- That love, even when wounded, can build something immortal.

Yes, dreams are heavy. But they are also holy. They remind you that life is not about drifting safely in calm waters; it is about daring to sail into storms, knowing the waves might break you, but believing you can rise again.

And Samarth rose. He rose until one day his daughter stood on an international stage, holding an award that bore both her name and his. In her voice, in her strength, in her dreams, his weight was finally lifted-not because it disappeared, but because it had transformed.

The weight of his dream had turned into wings for another.

So let this be his message to you:

Do not be afraid of the weight of your dream. If it feels heavy, it means it matters. If it matters, it is worth every sleepless night, every sacrifice, every shadow you face.

Because in the end, the ones who change the world are not those who run from the weight, but those who carry it-step by step, day by day-until the dream is no longer a burden, but a legacy.

Facing the First Betrayal

The crack in Samarth's faith did not come from an enemy's hand. It came from a man he had called brother. This was not just a colleague—this was someone Samarth had lifted up, trained, and trusted with his dreams. They had sat side by side through endless nights, sketching visions on the backs of napkins, speaking of empires, of books that would change classrooms, of futures built with honesty.

And yet, betrayal had been sitting quietly in the room all along.

It began with numbers—always numbers. Samarth, restless one evening, sat at his desk with the ledger open, the pen tapping against the page like a metronome of unease. A single entry seemed off. Then another. His brows knotted, his breath shallow. He recalculated. Once. Twice. A third time. Each time the truth pressed sharper against him: money had been siphoned.

"No… it has to be a mistake," he muttered, flipping pages, his voice growing tighter, almost desperate. "Not him. Not *him*."

But numbers do not lie, and that night they became executioners.

When he confronted the man, Samarth's chest still held a thin thread of hope—that there would be remorse, or at least shame. Instead, he received a shrug.

"Business mein aisa hota hai, Samarth. Don't take it personally."

The words landed like a slap. Cold. Casual. Cruel.

Samarth stared, mouth dry, trying to find language for the storm rising inside him. His voice cracked when it finally came out:

"You call this business? You call this friendship?"

But the man had already turned away, indifferent, as though trust itself were a currency too cheap to value.

That night, Samarth stayed alone in the office. The tube light flickered, throwing shadows across the walls like mocking silhouettes. The air was heavy with the smell of stale tea and ink. Papers lay scattered on the desk—plans, accounts, dreams—suddenly looking fragile, childish. He leaned back in his chair, tilting his head to the ceiling, eyes burning until the blur turned into tears he would not let fall freely.

"Why does everyone I trust break me?" he whispered into the hum of the dying tube light. The silence that followed was brutal, like an empty hall where even echoes had abandoned him.

Days dragged on. He smiled at clients, shook hands at meetings, but inside his fists clenched against invisible walls. Nights became battlegrounds—sleep fractured, mind replaying the shrug, the smirk, the dismissal. He wondered if he was cursed, if love and loyalty were flaws branded onto him from birth, open doors for exploitation.

Yet grief is a double-edged teacher. One side cuts, the other carves.

Through the haze, clarity emerged. He began to see betrayal not as a full stop, but as a colon—an opening for what came after. He told himself:

- Money lost can be earned again.
- Trust broken teaches you where to place it next.
- Scars, though ugly, can harden into armour.

And so, he rebuilt. Brick by brick, page by page. He checked accounts with surgical precision. He demanded transparency like a creed. Faith remained in him, but it was sharpened, no longer blind.

Years later, when Misha once asked why he always studied people so long before trusting them, Samarth paused, the old wound flickering in his eyes. He smiled faintly, touched her hair, and said: "Because once, beta, I trusted blindly. And it almost destroyed me. But I also learnt—when you find loyalty that is true, you never let it slip away."

The betrayal had not erased him. It had reforged him. What was once a wound had become armour. And beneath that armour, his heart still beat—not weaker, but wiser.

Betrayal by Nature

If betrayal by a man had shaken Samarth's faith, the second betrayal arrived from a place no one could fight—nature itself. *Covid-19* swept across the globe like a storm without sound, and Samarth's company, built around classrooms and learning, found itself standing on broken ground.

Overnight, schools shut their doors. Projects that were once his lifeline were suddenly "on hold until further notice." Invoices went unpaid, contracts were frozen, and the steady rhythm of cash flow that had kept the company alive fell silent like a stopped heartbeat.

The boardroom, once alive with plans and visions,

turned into a battlefield of survival. The numbers on the whiteboard no longer spoke of expansion, only of how long the company could last before the tank ran dry. For the first time in years, Samarth felt the suffocating weight of helplessness pressing against his chest.

But when the suggestion came—cut staff to reduce expenses—Samarth refused without hesitation. "Not one person will be thrown out," he said, his voice trembling but firm. "We built this together, we will survive this together." His team's eyes filled with tears, because in that moment, they understood: their leader would bleed before he let them drown.

And bleed he did.

Samarth sold his beloved XUV, the car that had once carried him through the streets of Lucknow like a badge of triumph. He walked into the bank with Ruhi's jewellery wrapped in a small cloth pouch, his hands shaking as he placed them on the counter. Every piece of gold was a memory—a wedding, a festival, a moment of joy—and yet here they were, reduced to collateral for survival. Signing the papers felt like carving chunks off his pride, but Samarth's face did not flinch. His team's families depended on him, and that was a burden he refused to drop.

Nights became the cruelest. When the children

were asleep and the house quiet, Samarth sat alone on the balcony, staring into the deserted streets, his head bowed. Tears often came uninvited, and though he tried to hide them from Ruhi, she would sometimes find him, broken and silent. She would sit beside him, place a hand on his shoulder, and whisper, "We will get through this." It was her strength, as much as his, that kept the fire alive.

Covid dragged on longer than anyone imagined. Every month was a new mountain to climb—vendors calling, staff growing anxious, creditors pressing harder. And yet, every month, somehow, salaries were paid, even if smaller, and no one was abandoned. Samarth bore the weight like a man bracing against a flood—battered, exhausted, but unyielding.

Betrayal by Blood

But storms rarely come alone. As Samarth battled nature, he turned to family for help, believing that when the world collapses, blood will hold you up. What he found instead was another scar.

His cousin brother on the maternal side, someone who had once laughed with him at family gatherings, now became a gatekeeper of power. "If you want a loan," he said coolly, "make a full presentation. Show us your growth projections, your survival strategy.

Convince us why you deserve it."

Samarth, exhausted yet desperate, poured himself into the task. Night after night, he sat before the glow of his laptop, building slides with trembling hands, numbers blurring before his tired eyes. He rehearsed every line, crafted every chart, shaping not just a presentation but a plea from his heart. He was not asking as an entrepreneur—he was asking as family.

When the day came, he presented with all the passion left in him. But in the end, it was all a cruel charade. His cousin had never intended to help. The effort was brushed aside with vague smiles and mocking words: "We'll think about it." Hours, days, energy—all wasted.

Worse, others joined in with harsher terms. "We'll invest," some said, "but only if you give us 50 to 60 percent equity." His company, his blood and sweat, reduced to a bargaining chip.

That night, Samarth sat silently beside Ruhi, his heart heavy. She touched his shoulder gently, asking without words. He finally whispered, "I thought family would save me. Instead, they showed me how powerless they think I am." His voice broke, but behind his tears, steel was forming.

He learned then: some doors stay closed not because you lack the key, but because opening them would empty your house.

Betrayal by Power

If betrayal by blood was bitter, betrayal by power was venomous. Dixit, a wealthy industry expert and once Samarth's boss, came forward during the crisis with an offer that looked like rescue. "I will invest five million rupees," he said smoothly, "but it will be a loan at interest. And—I want an administrative role in your company."

Samarth's chest tightened. He needed the money desperately. Salaries had to be paid, vendors needed their dues, and the walls were closing in. He thought long and hard. The interest, though heavy, was something he could bear. But to hand over the reins of his company—the dream he had built brick by brick—to a man who cared only for control? That was a price too high.

He had worked under Dixit once. He knew the man's kind: men who never wanted subordinates to rise, who built walls around their own power and crushed anyone who dared to climb higher. Such people never invested to support; they invested to break, to block, to suffocate ambition.

At last, with reluctance but resolve, Samarth agreed only to the interest-based loan. He refused to give away control. That decision saved him. For Dixit was never truly an ally—he was a predator circling weakness.

When he realised he could not take over, he vanished, leaving Samarth stranded once more, exposed to the storm.

For days after, Samarth's heart burned with humiliation. Help had been dangled before him only to remind him of his place. Yet even this betrayal became another scar on his armour.

He kept walking. Sometimes the only victory is to keep walking.

The Season of Betrayals

The season that followed became the harshest winter of Samarth's life—a time when warmth was stolen again and again, leaving behind scars that would mark him forever.

The first wound came from **man**—a colleague he had called brother. Together they had built dreams on paper napkins, drawn castles in air, and whispered about futures brimming with honesty. Yet when greed entered the room, trust was the first to be sacrificed. Numbers on a ledger became knives, and the shrug of indifference cut deeper than any blade.

That betrayal left Samarth hollow, teaching him that sometimes the face across the table wears friendship like a mask while chiselling away at your soul.

No sooner had he staggered from that wound

than another arrived—this time from nature. Covid descended like a shadow without mercy. Schools shut, contracts froze, and his company's veins ran dry. Every day was a reckoning: pay rent or pay salaries, choose vendors or choose survival. The easiest path was to cut people loose, but Samarth refused. Instead, he bled himself dry—selling his beloved XUV, pawning Ruhi's jewellery, walking into banks with trembling hands but an unbending will.

At night, when the children slept, he wept quietly on the balcony, the silence broken only by Ruhi's hand on his shoulder. That betrayal was not born of malice but of fate—and yet, it carved into him the deepest scar: the helplessness of carrying lives on your back when your own knees are shaking.

As if the storm were not enough, betrayal arrived from **blood**. His cousin brother on the maternal side, who had once shared childhood laughter, now sat across the table like a stranger. "Make a presentation if you want help," he demanded, his voice laced with superiority.

Samarth worked through nights, building slides with trembling hands, rehearsing numbers like a desperate student before an exam. But it was all a cruel play—the help never came. Worse, others in the family circled like vultures, demanding half the company in exchange for survival. What hurt was not their refusal—it was their hunger to profit from his pain.

That betrayal taught him that blood ties can sometimes bind tighter around your neck than around your heart.

And then came betrayal by **power**. Dixit, his former boss, a man wealthy and revered in the industry, approached like a saviour. "I'll invest five million," he said smoothly, "but at interest—and I want an administrative role." Samarth knew his type.

He had once worked under him, seen how men like him never lifted subordinates up but pressed them down, guarding their thrones. For days, Samarth wrestled with the offer. The money was needed, desperately. The interest he could bear, but to hand over his company—the sweat of his life—to a man who would choke it for pride? That he could not do.

When Samarth refused to yield control, Dixit vanished, leaving him stranded. That betrayal showed him how power often extends a hand only to pull you further into chains.

Four betrayals. Four scars.

Each one stripped something from him—comfort, pride, illusions, even trust. He was tested by greed, by fate, by family, and by those who once called themselves leaders. He was left standing in the middle of the storm, his arms empty, but his spirit still defiant.

Samarth mortgaged his property, borrowed at punishing interest, and invested every last rupee back into the company. Covid lasted longer than anyone predicted, stretching hope until it felt like glass about to shatter. And yet, month after month, he paid salaries, cleared vendor dues, and kept the wheel turning when others collapsed.

When the fog finally lifted, his company still stood—not untouched, not pristine, but alive. And so did he.

The scars remained. They always would. But scars are not just wounds—they are armour. Each betrayal had cut him, but each cut had healed into steel.

Samarth emerged not bitter, but forged in fire. Stronger. Harder. Wiser.

Empty Wallet, Heavy Heart

There were months when the company's bank balance scraped the bottom. Payments from clients were delayed, creditors called every day with voices sharp with impatience, and expenses piled higher than the thin stack of receipts. Salaries were due, and the numbers on the ledger looked like wounds that refused to close.

In those moments, Samarth faced the decision every leader dreads: *who gets paid, and who must wait?*

His answer was clear. He paid his employees first. To him, they were not just workers; they were families with mouths to feed, children whose school fees couldn't wait, and dreams that could collapse if he failed. He chose to protect them, even if it meant walking home with empty pockets.

So he went home empty-handed. He folded the same old shirts, avoided shop windows that glittered with new clothes, skipped dinners out, and quietly told himself, *This is only temporary.*

But he could not hide everything. His wife noticed, as she always did. One evening, when the house was quiet and the table was heavy with bills, she placed her hand gently on his.

"Samarth," she whispered, "even if you have nothing, we are with you."

Those words broke through his defences. He turned his face away so she wouldn't see the tears burning in his eyes. He wasn't crying because of poverty. He was crying because of love. To have someone stand with you when the world calls you a fool-that is the kind of wealth no bank can measure.

It was in these seasons of emptiness that Samarth understood the real weight of entrepreneurship. It wasn't about titles, profits, or the applause of outsiders. It was about carrying storms on your shoulders, with an umbrella full of holes, and still choosing to walk forward. It was about saying *yes* to tomorrow when today gave you nothing.

And so, he endured:

- He renegotiated contracts with humility and firmness.
- He called on old clients, not begging, but reminding them that loyalty should outlast delays.
- He cut every unnecessary cost, teaching his team the discipline of survival.
- And when the nights stretched long and silent, he reminded himself why he began: to build something that mattered, something that would live longer than his struggles.

An empty wallet did not mean an empty future.

Slowly, the tide shifted. Payments trickled in. Salaries were met on time. The lights in the office stayed on, not because of magic, but because of a leader's stubborn faith. Each storm survived became another brick in the fortress of his resolve. Each sacrifice turned into a story of strength he carried silently.

Years later, Misha would hear these stories. Sometimes from her father, sometimes whispered by loyal employees who remembered those days vividly. She would sit wide-eyed, listening to how her father had gone hungry so his staff could eat, how he had worn old shirts so others could buy schoolbooks for their children.

One evening, while studying abroad, she called him after a long and exhausting day. "Papa," she said, "how did you do it? How did you carry so much?"

Samarth chuckled softly, though his eyes glistened. "Beta, when your dream is bigger than your hunger, you find a way. And when people depend on you, you don't ask *if* it's possible-you make it possible."

Those words became a compass for her. When she later faced her own storms-doubts in boardrooms, clients swayed by competitors, challenges larger than her youth-she remembered her father's empty wallet and his heavy heart. She remembered that courage is not the absence of fear, but the choice to rise despite it.

And when she stood on international stages, when the company's name reached beyond borders, Misha carried her father's sacrifices with her like invisible wings. Every achievement of hers was rooted in those nights of scarcity. Every accolade was built on the quiet heroism of a man who once walked home empty-handed, but never empty-hearted.

Because this is the truth:

Entrepreneurs are not the ones who never fall. They are the ones who fall, break, bleed, and still rise-because they know their dream is not theirs alone.

Samarth's empty wallet built not just a company, but a daughter's strength.

And his heavy heart became the foundation of a legacy that will never run dry.

The Loneliness of Leadership

Leadership is the loneliest summit a man can climb. To the world, it gleams with authority, prestige, and applause. But Samarth knew the view from the top was not splendour—it was silence. Behind the polished shoes and well-timed smile lay a hollow that no one else could see.

Employees brought him their anxieties. Clients brought him their impatience. Family brought him their faith. Everyone leaned on him, expecting answers, expecting strength. But who was there to hold his trembling? Where could he take the raw weight of his own grief?

At night, when duty finally loosened its grip, Samarth would mount his bike and surrender himself to the dark. The city emptied as he rode—streets that in the day bustled with ambition now lay deserted, echoing only with the roar of his engine. Wind tore at his face, stripping away the armour he wore by day. He let the tears stream unchecked; the night, mercifully, did not ask questions.

Sometimes his journey ended by the riverbank, where the water lay black and restless. Samarth would sit on the stone embankment, arms folded, eyes fixed on the surface that reflected only his unrest.

"Ayush," he whispered once, voice cracking, "if you were here, I would not be so alone. You would laugh, you would tease, you would push me forward. Even silence would feel lighter with you beside me."

He closed his eyes and, for a fleeting second, saw it: Ayush bounding into his office with files in hand, filling the room with careless jokes, brainstorming ideas with youthful fervour, banishing the air of fatigue that clung to Samarth's shoulders. The vision made him smile, then broke him all over again. For imagination was all that remained.

That was the cruel paradox of leadership: to lift everyone else, he had to conceal his own collapse. He steadied trembling voices when his own shook. He nodded to reassure clients while doubting himself. He smiled at his family even as emptiness chewed through him. Leadership was not glamour; it was endurance disguised as grace.

And yet, the same loneliness that scalded him also chiselled him. It forced him to strip away illusions, to stop seeking strength in applause or company, and to turn inward. Night after night, Samarth discovered the strange alchemy of pain—how tears could be refined into resolve, how grief could stiffen into grit.

One night by the river, as the moon floated above like a pale witness, Samarth whispered into the stillness:

"If loneliness must be my companion, then let it sharpen me, not shatter me. If I must walk without Ayush, then I will walk carrying him within me."

When dawn returned, so did Samarth—back in his office, tie knotted, voice calm, shoulders squared. His team never guessed that their shield was a man stitched together by sleepless nights. They only saw his steadiness, not the fracture beneath.

This, Samarth realised, was the true anatomy of leadership:

- To bleed unseen, yet heal others openly.
- To break at night, yet inspire at dawn.
- To carry a scar that throbs, yet still build something that endures.

Ayush's absence would never be filled. But Samarth chose to carry it as proof of love, as memory made flesh, as purpose burning in silence.

From the riverbanks of grief, he learnt the hardest lesson of all: Great leaders are not those spared loneliness. Great leaders are those who take loneliness, cradle it, and turn it into light for others to follow.

The Daughter's Innocence

In those days of despair, when betrayal stung and grief pressed against his ribs like a weight that refused to lift, Misha became his unexpected anchor. She was still a child, yet her words often carried the gravity of an old soul.

One evening, Samarth sat at the dining table long after the plates had been cleared, his elbows on the wood, his head buried in his hands. The fan hummed lazily overhead, the night outside heavy with the scent of rain-soaked earth. He thought he was alone—thought his mask of strength had finally slipped in the privacy of the dark.

Then he felt small arms loop gently around his neck. Startled, he lifted his head. Misha stood there in her nightdress, her hair falling messily over her forehead, her eyes too large, too knowing for her age.

"Papa," she whispered, pressing her cheek to his shoulder, "don't be sad. One day you will have the biggest company in the world."

Samarth let out a shaky laugh through his tears. "And why, little madam, are you so sure of that?"

She pulled back, her face earnest. "Because you're my hero."

The simplicity of it struck him harder than any

boardroom applause ever had. He blinked, trying to hide his tears, but Misha caught them. She reached up with her small hand and clumsily wiped his cheek.

"Heroes are not supposed to cry," she said with the blunt honesty only a child could manage.

"Even heroes cry, beta," Samarth replied softly, kissing her forehead. "That's how they remember they're human."

"But you'll still win, Papa," she insisted, her voice firm now, almost commanding. "You always do. I know it."

Her certainty lodged itself deep inside him, like a seed that refused to die. That single sentence—you're my hero—became his shield. Whenever fatigue whispered, whenever doubts circled like vultures, he heard her voice again, clear as temple bells in his memory.

In the days that followed, he found himself walking into meetings straighter, speaking firmer, smiling more. Not because the pain had lessened, but because a little girl had reminded him of who he was—not broken, not defeated, but a hero in her eyes.

And sometimes, when the nights grew heavy again, he would whisper back to the shadows:

"If my daughter can believe in me, then I must believe in myself."

Breaking Point

One evening, after a brutal day of rejections and mounting bills, Samarth stayed late in the office. The city outside buzzed with indifferent life, but his small office was silent. Papers lay scattered like fallen leaves. The tube light flickered, throwing jittery shadows across the walls.

He picked up his phone and stared at Ayush's old number, still saved. Tears blurred his vision. "Beta," he whispered into the stillness, "why did you leave me to fight this alone?"

The sobs came then, raw and unrestrained. For a few moments, he allowed himself to collapse under the weight he carried every day.

And then, in the dim hum of the flickering light, his father's voice returned—steady, unwavering, like a hand on his shoulder from another world.

Papa's Voice

"Samarth," it said, calm but firm, "you give too much of yourself to people who only know how to take."

Samarth lifted his face, streaked with tears. "But Papa, if even family leaves you, then what is the point of sacrifice?"

The reply came, quiet but cutting through the fog: "The point is not whether they stay or leave. The point is who *you* become in the giving. Sacrifice is not a bargain, Samarth—it is your truth. Do not let their silence corrupt your nature."

Samarth's voice cracked, almost pleading. "But I am tired, Papa. Tired of carrying everyone, tired of fighting alone."

His father's voice grew steadier, stronger:

"Then fight for yourself. Fight for your wife. For Misha. For the children who look to you. For the company you built from dust. Let their betrayal harden you, not break you. Remember—steel is born only in fire."

Samarth shut his eyes, breathing heavily. "And if the fire consumes me, Papa?"

"Then you rise from the ashes," came the reply, "because you are not made of clay—you are made of flame."

Resolution

The words echoed in him, sharper than any scripture.

Samarth wiped his tears, his breath still ragged but his chest slowly steadying. He stood up, fists clenched, whispering fiercely into the empty office:

"No. If they want me to fail, I will succeed. If life has broken me, I will rise broken. And from these cracks, light will come."

The Recurring Voice

From that night onward, whenever despair pressed too hard, Papa's words would return—sometimes as rebuke, sometimes as comfort, but always as compass.

When colleagues turned petty, he heard: *"Do not bend to their smallness. Keep your eyes on the larger road."*

When loneliness dragged him toward bitterness, he heard: *"Do not let grief rot into hate. Let it sharpen into wisdom."*

When the weight of leadership suffocated him, he heard: *"You are not alone. My blood runs in you. Stand."*

And slowly, Samarth understood: his father had not left. He lived on, as voice, as conscience, as the unyielding fire within.

Breakthroughs

Pain had honed him. Betrayal had taught him caution. Loneliness had forged resilience.

And then—slowly, almost imperceptibly—the cracks began to let light in. A major order was confirmed. A school signed a long-term contract. Cash flow, once a suffocating trickle, steadied and grew. Salaries were paid on time.

The very employees who once feared collapse now looked at him with awe. They whispered among themselves, "Sir doesn't just run this place—he carries us all on his shoulders."

Samarth did not boast. He did not need to. His victories spoke in their own clear voice. Yet, in the privacy of his mind, every contract signed, every cheque cleared, carried the same whispered dedication: *This one's for you, Ayush.*

The Catharsis

One evening, after closing a deal that once seemed impossible, Samarth returned home quietly. His wife greeted him with a knowing smile, sensing a shift in the air. Misha bounded into his arms, her small voice eager: "Papa, how was your day?"

He hugged her tightly, too overcome to answer. Tears spilled—not of pain this time, but of release, like a storm finally breaking after years of drought. And beneath his breath, unheard by anyone else, he murmured, "Did you see that, Ayush? We did it."

In that moment, Samarth realised something deeper than success: it was not measured in money or applause, but in endurance. It was about surviving the nights when surrender seemed easier than hope, and still showing up the next morning. Success was not about strength alone—it was about the faith of those who believed in you, and the unseen eyes you still longed to make proud.

Reflection

This journey was never just about business. It was about life's most brutal lessons.

Samarth had endured betrayal from partners, silence from family, the emptiness of unpaid bills, and nights that splintered him into fragments. He had wept in secret, screamed in loneliness, pleaded with fate. And yet, he rose.

He rose because his wife's faith refused to waver.

He rose because his daughter's innocence gave him courage.

He rose because of the memory of Ayush—his nephew who would never grow old. In moments of triumph, Samarth often closed his eyes and pictured Ayush sitting in the front row, clapping wildly, teasing him afterward with that mischievous grin: "Chachu, ab toh aap hero ban gaye." ("Uncle, now you've become the hero.") The applause of the living never felt as full as the imagined claps of the one who was gone.

And he rose because, even broken, he carried within him a spirit that would not surrender.

By the time he looked back, the world saw him as a successful entrepreneur. But he knew the truth: every brick of his company was cemented not only with money, but with tears, scars, sleepless nights, and the dedication of a man who built as if Ayush were still watching.

If you looked closely at the walls of his office, you would not just see paint and plaster. You would see testimony—the faint laughter of Ayush woven into the fabric of its success, mingling with the grit of a man betrayed, abandoned, broken—and still, somehow, choosing to rise.

Chapter 9

New Philosophy of Success – Living With Scars, Leading With Heart

The Calm After the Storm

There comes a moment in every man's life when he realises success is not about how high you climb, but about how deeply you survive.

For Samarth, that moment did not arrive with applause, a fat contract, or his name in print. It came quietly—on an ordinary morning, as he stood barefoot in his prayer room after lighting a small lamp. Through the half-open window, the city stirred awake. The flame quivered, the incense curled, and beyond the smoke, the skyline glittered with towers of ambition.

He watched the world below—traffic inching forward, people hurrying to offices, children tugging at schoolbags. Each figure seemed like a soul chasing shadows, restless, urgent. Once, he had been one of them—rushing, proving, straining against clocks. But after everything—the betrayals, the drought of money, the long nights of solitude, and most painfully, Ayush's absence—he no longer rushed.

For the first time, he allowed himself to simply stand still. The stillness was prayer, and in that silence he discovered clarity. It was as if the lamp's small flame whispered: *endurance is worship, patience is strength, and love is the only true wealth.*

Success Redefined

In his early years, success had been a scoreboard: contracts bagged, targets crossed, trophies displayed like armour.

Now, it meant something else entirely:

- Success was paying his employees on time, knowing their children would sleep with full stomachs.
- Success was coming home early, sitting cross-legged while Misha shared her school stories, his mind fully hers.
- Success was holding his wife's hand in silence, feeling a bond beyond words.
- Success was choosing peace over pride, boundaries over blind sacrifice.

He saw now that the world glorifies wealth and power, but the truest currency of life is love—given wisely, guarded with reverence.

Scars as Strength

Samarth carried scars. Some carved by betrayal, others by unreturned sacrifice, and one—the deepest—by Ayush's absence.

For years he had hidden them, ashamed, as though they were failures. But now he realised they were not marks of weakness—they were scriptural lines etched into his body, verses of survival.

When a young employee once murmured, "Sir, I feel broken. I don't think I can rise again," Samarth rolled up his sleeve, tapped the faint scar on his arm, then placed a palm over his chest.

"These are my wounds," he said softly. "Life cut me open. But every scar proves one thing: I am still standing. And if I can stand, so can you."

The boy's eyes filled, and in that instant, Samarth knew: vulnerability was no longer a private burden. It had become a gift he could offer others.

Boundaries of Love

The hardest lesson came not from business, but from family.

Samarth once thought love meant endless sacrifice. He gave without limit, until betrayal made him understand: love without wisdom leads to self-destruction.

Now, he gave with awareness. He helped with limits. He learnt to say no. Not out of bitterness, but out of clarity.

When a cousin asked for financial help for the third time in six months, Samarth listened, then smiled gently.

"I will guide you," he said, "but I cannot carry you. You must walk too."

It was firm, but kind. And in that moment he saw how far he had come—from a man who lost himself in giving, to a man who gave with discernment.

Later that night, unable to sleep, Samarth climbed to the roof. The city stretched before him, restless and glittering, each light a reminder of how crowded the world could be and yet how lonely it often felt. He tilted his face to the sky, where the stars burned cold and indifferent.

"Ayush," he whispered, voice unsteady, "do you see me still trying? Do you see me learning how to live differently? I thought love meant giving until I bled. Now I know love must also protect itself. Would you have understood that, beta?"

The wind moved around him like a quiet answer. For a long time, he stood there, speaking softly into the night—not for the city to hear, but for the boy he still carried in his heart.

That morning, as the lamp's flame flickered in the prayer room, Samarth bowed his head. For the first time, he felt not just like a man who had survived, but like a man who had been renewed. His scars were his scriptures. His love, bounded and wise, was his prayer. And his stillness—after the storm—was his truest success.

The Daughter as His Compass

If scars were Samarth's teachers, Misha was his compass.

Every major decision—whether to expand into new markets, to accept an international offer, or to spend another night at work—was weighed against a single question: How will this affect her?

When tempted with a lucrative contract that demanded long travel, he refused. "I will not trade my daughter's childhood for another zero in my account," he told himself.

He watched her grow—her laughter filling the house, her drawings pinned proudly to the fridge, her words often carrying a clarity beyond her years. Once, she told her friends at school, "My papa is my hero. Not because he works hard, but because he always comes home for dinner."

In that moment, Samarth knew he had chosen the right compass. She reminded him daily that life was not about blind ambition. It was about presence. About being human. About being love itself.

Leadership With Heart

At work, Samarth's leadership softened into something deeper. He was no longer just the strategist or the deal-closer. He became the leader who remembered birthdays, who asked after ageing parents, who sent weary employees home early.

When one staff member once broke down in his office over personal struggles, Samarth didn't lecture about professionalism. Instead, he poured a cup of tea, pushed it across the table, and said quietly:

"Take your time. I know what it means to cry in silence."

That simple act built more loyalty than any incentive scheme ever could. His team didn't just work for him—they believed in him. They stayed late not out of fear, but out of faith, choosing to walk beside him.

And when outsiders asked, "What is it like working under Samarth sir?" the answer was always the same:

"It doesn't feel like working under him. It feels like working with him."

Conversations With Ayush

In his quietest hours, when the house finally surrendered to silence and even the ceiling fan seemed to hesitate in its turning, Samarth found himself in conversation with Ayush. These were not spoken aloud like ordinary talk, but whispered across the stillness of night—half prayer, half memory, like a father reaching across worlds.

"Beta, are you watching? Do you see what I'm building? I hope you are proud…"

He would sit at his desk long after everyone else had drifted into sleep, the lamp throwing a weary pool of light across scattered files. In those moments, he imagined Ayush leaning against the doorway, hands in his pockets, that familiar mischievous smile tilting his face.

In his vision, Ayush chuckled softly, shaking his head.

"Chachu, you work too much. You'll go grey before your time. Don't frown so hard at those numbers—they're not life, they're only ink."

Sometimes Samarth imagined him spinning playfully in the office chair, legs swinging, tossing out ideas with the reckless ease of youth.

"Why don't you try this? Or that? Take risks, Chachu. You always play safe. Life isn't meant to be lived with so many locks on the door."

Samarth would close his eyes, letting the echo of that imagined voice seep through his bones. Tears often blurred the ink on his papers, but strangely, those tears steadied him.

There were nights when the weight of it all threatened to crush him—when payments stalled, when faith ran thin, when the future seemed no more than a fog. On those nights, he touched Ayush's photograph and whispered: "Help me, beta. Lend me your courage. Remind me why I fight."

And in some unseen, unexplainable way, he felt lighter. It was as though Ayush's spirit leaned across the divide, placed a hand on his shoulder, and said with quiet insistence:

"You're not alone, Chachu. I'm still here. Don't stop. Keep building. Keep living."

The grief never dulled; it never could. But it changed shape. It became a presence rather than an absence—a companion that hurt, but also held him up. Every ache reminded Samarth of the love that ran so deep it could defy death itself.

The Dream

One night, exhaustion carried him into a dream so vivid it felt like waking. He stood on the rooftop of his childhood home in Ranchi, the stars spread wide and trembling above. A cool wind brushed his face.

And there—leaning casually against the parapet—stood Ayush. Not pale, not silent, but full of life: eyes bright, hair tousled, his smile carrying that old defiance of sorrow.

"Chachu," Ayush said, as if no years had passed, "you've become too serious. You carry the world on your shoulders, but you forget—it doesn't need to be carried alone."

Samarth's throat tightened. He wanted to speak, but words stuck. At last, his voice broke through:

"Why did you leave me, beta? Why did you go before I could show you everything I dreamt for you?"

Ayush's gaze softened. He stepped closer, placing a hand on Samarth's arm. The touch felt real, warm.

"I didn't leave you, Chachu. I just walk in a place you can't see. Every time you rise, I rise with you. Every time you choose love over bitterness, you honour me."

Samarth wept, the tears hot and unashamed. "I miss you every day."

Ayush smiled gently. "Then keep missing me—but don't stop living. Build what you dreamed. Take care of Misha. And when you look at the stars, know I'm watching too."

The dream dissolved in dawn's first light. Samarth awoke with wet cheeks, his chest aching but lighter, as if some invisible weight had shifted. The rooftop was gone, the stars replaced by the dim glow of his desk lamp. But Ayush's words lingered like incense-smoke, curling, fading, yet refusing to vanish.

Once, Misha found him sitting before Ayush's picture, his fingers resting gently on the frame.

"Papa," she asked softly, "do you still talk to him?"

Samarth's throat tightened. He swallowed hard before answering.

"Every day, beta," he said quietly. "Because some conversations never end. Not even when the person is gone."

And so, Samarth carried on—living, building, loving—his nights stitched with conversations across the unseen. For even in absence, Ayush was still guiding him, still shaping him, still walking beside him in the only way love knows how: eternally.

Chapter 10

A Father's Heart, A Daughter's World -Where Love Becomes Legacy

The Centre of His Universe

After Ayush's death, Samarth's heart was scarred, but not hollow. Into that scar, love for his daughter Misha poured like sunlight through a broken window.

He had always loved her, but now, she became his reason to keep breathing. Every laugh of hers became a rope pulling him out of despair. Every question she asked reminded him that the world, though cruel, was still alive.

Misha didn't know it then, but she had saved him. And he made her the center of his universe.

"Papa, are you okay?" she asked one evening, her tiny hand on his knee.

Samarth forced a smile. "If you are okay, beta, then I am okay."

It wasn't a lie. For him, her happiness was the measure of his survival.

Lessons in Strength

Misha was not just a daughter, she was a prayer answered. Long before she was born, Samarth had whispered to God, "***Give me a girl, not a boy. Give me someone I can protect, and someone who will teach me tenderness.***" When Misha arrived, small and fragile in his arms, he felt the universe had placed a jewel in his palm. From that day forward, she became his lifeline, his reason to hope, his reason to fight, his reason to keep breathing when grief tried to crush him.

Samarth had long believed the world was unfair, especially to women. He had seen it everywhere: in boardrooms where men spoke over brilliant women, in households where daughters were weighed like burdens instead of blessings. He swore his Misha would never live bent under the weight of someone else's expectations.

And so, he taught her early:

- To ride a bicycle, even if her knees bled on the gravel.
- To speak her mind at the dinner table, even if the elders frowned.
- To look people in the eye when she said *"no."*
- To dream without apology, and to dream beyond the cages others might build for her.

One evening, when Misha returned home with tears rolling down her cheeks because a classmate had mocked her handwriting, Samarth found her curled in a corner, clutching her notebook. He sat beside her, took out a blank sheet of paper, and wrote slowly. His letters sprawled awkwardly, uneven, a far cry from perfection.

"See this?" he chuckled, holding up the page. "Even Papa doesn't write perfectly."

Her tears broke into laughter, shaky but real. He wiped her face with his thumb and kissed her hair. Then he whispered words she would carry like a secret prayer: *"Strength, beta, is not about never crying. It is about standing up after you cry."*

From that day, Misha wore those words like invisible armour. In school, in friendships, in her own private battles, she carried the mantra her father had given her. To Samarth, she was more than a daughter-she was the wish that had come true, the reason he could survive the storms, the reminder that even in a world of loss and cruelty, love could still create strength.

She was not only his child. She was his anchor, his lifeline, the beating heart that kept him from sinking.

The Little Rituals

Samarth made fatherhood into an art of rituals-small,

imperfect, but stitched with love so deep that they became the fabric of Misha's childhood.

- **Morning walks**, when the world was still half-asleep, became their secret corridor. As dew clung to grass and the city yawned awake, she told him her dreams, her fears, her silly jokes. He listened as though every word was scripture.
- **Sunday breakfasts** turned into family legends. He could not cook well, his parathas were often burnt at the edges, sometimes raw in the middle but he served them proudly. And Misha ate them with exaggerated delight, knowing it wasn't the taste but the ritual that mattered.
- **Evening bike rides** were their private carnival. Her small arms wrapped tightly around his waist, her laughter carried by the wind. "Faster, Papa!" she shouted, and he pedalled harder, as though joy itself was chasing them.

He wove love into moments so ordinary that they became extraordinary. Every exam day, he stood outside the hall, waiting with a chocolate hidden in his pocket. It was never about the marks; it was his way of saying, *"No matter the result, I am here."*

Every birthday, instead of expensive gifts, he gave her letters. Letters that became lanterns she would carry into her growing years. In one, he wrote: *"My dear Misha, be the girl who lifts others when they fall, but never forget to hold yourself first."*

She pressed those letters between the pages of her notebooks, like fragile petals she wanted to preserve. Even as she grew older, the ritual never faded. She returned to those words on days when life tested her, and each time, they gave her back her strength.

To Samarth, these rituals were never small. They were the threads that bound him to the daughter he had once prayed for, the girl he had asked God to place in his life. And to Misha, they were proof that love did not need grandeur-it only needed presence.

Because in the end, it was not the parathas or the chocolates that mattered, but the certainty they carried: *that she was seen, she was treasured, and she was never alone.*

The Quiet Sacrifices

Samarth's career was a corridor lined with temptations, foreign postings, prestigious titles, lucrative jobs that promised him the world. Colleagues shook their heads, whispering he was foolish to let such chances pass. Relatives mocked his "lack of ambition," reminding him how many fathers would have seized the opportunity.

But ambition, for Samarth, was something else entirely. It was not measured in designations or foreign trips. It was measured in *presence*.

When Misha was small, her world was stitched together by moments she never wanted to forget and Samarth wanted to be there for every single one of them. He wanted to be the face in the audience when she recited her first poem, his applause rising above the rest. He wanted to cheer when she stumbled across a finish line with her first medal, even if it was just for a school sports day. He wanted to hold her tiny hand as he walked her to the school gate each morning, listening to her chatter about crayons, friends, and the stories she had dreamt the night before.

While other fathers were continents away chasing promotions, Samarth bent down to tie her shoelaces, sat cross-legged on the floor helping her finish school projects, and carried her on his shoulders when her little legs grew tired. These were his boardrooms; these were his triumphs.

He gave up promotions that would have taken him far from home. He let go of bonuses that glittered with promises but would have cost him evenings of laughter and mornings of school runs. He turned his back on global recognition because he knew medals and titles fade, but a child's memory of her father being there never does.

And he never once regretted it.

For Samarth, success was not stamped on certificates or etched on brass nameplates. It was reflected in Misha's smile when she spotted him in a crowd. It was carried in her voice when she shouted, "Papa, did you see me?" and he could always answer, truthfully, *"Yes, beta. I saw everything."*

His life was her life. His ambition was her smile. His quiet sacrifices, invisible to the world, built the loudest, strongest foundation of love.

Graduation Dreams

As Misha grew, so did her dreams. She no longer looked only at the lanes of her city-she looked at the world. She wanted to study abroad, to test herself against challenges larger than the comfort of home, to step into a life her father could only imagine.

One evening, in a hesitant whisper, she said, *"Papa, I want to study in the UK."* Her voice trembled, as though the words themselves carried guilt, as if her dream might weigh too heavily on her father's shoulders.

Samarth took her hand without hesitation and said simply, *"Then UK it is."*

She blinked at him in disbelief. *"But Papa… it's too expensive."*

He smiled, his eyes carrying the quiet fire of a man who had lived on sacrifice. *"Beta, do you know what fathers are made of? Sacrifice stitched with love. Don't worry about the money, that's my work. Your only job is to fly."*

From that day on, every rupee he earned had a new destination, her future. He skipped comforts others called necessities, delayed his own dreams, and shelved personal plans without regret. Misha's dream became his project, her ambition his mission. Each bill paid, each form submitted, each sleepless night spent planning became a brick in the bridge he was building for her.

And when her acceptance letter arrived, Samarth felt as though his own childhood wish had finally come true-not for himself, but through her. His daughter was going to walk the roads he could only picture in books.

The Departure

The day she left for the UK, the airport transformed into a temple of emotions. Samarth carried her bags as though they were fragments of his own heart. He adjusted her scarf, checked her documents again and again, fussed over every small detail-just as he had on her very first school trip when she was a little girl with plaits and ribbons.

"Papa, I'll be fine," Misha said, her laughter breaking through her tears.

He cupped her cheek, his hand lingering. *"I know you'll be fine. But let me fuss. Fathers don't get many chances to show love. Let me hold on a little longer."*

When she disappeared past the security gates, swallowed by the crowd, Samarth stood frozen, eyes fixed on the place where he had last seen her. His chest ached with emptiness, but his eyes glistened with pride. He had sent his daughter into the world not just with education, but with the wings of his belief.

That evening, the house was quieter than it had ever been. Her room lay empty, her desk bare, the air carrying the ghost of her laughter. Samarth walked in, sat at her study table, and ran his fingers across the worn edges of her books. He closed his eyes, pressed his lips to the surface, and whispered into the silence:

"Live well, beta. Live the life I could not. Carry my dreams in your steps, and let the world know the strength of a daughter raised with love."

In that moment, Samarth realised: this was his graduation too, not with a cap and gown, but with the pride of seeing his greatest lesson fulfilled. His ambition was not a title, not a position. His ambition was Misha. And now, she was flying.

The Master's Degree

After completing her graduation, she earned a place in one of the UK's most prestigious business schools-the *UCL School of Business.* Her father, Samarth, encouraged her with words that carried both love and vision:

"Continue your Master's, my child. Learn the art of entrepreneurship, so that one day you may take charge of the company I have built. You will not only preserve it, you will scale it higher than I ever dreamed."

She carried those words with her through every lecture, every project, and every sleepless night of study. For her, the Master's program was more than education-it was preparation to carry forward a legacy.

When the day of her convocation arrived, the grand hall was filled with proud families, cheering classmates, and the music of triumph. As she walked across the stage in her black gown and cap, degree in hand, her eyes searched the audience.

There he was-Samarth. Sitting tall, eyes glistening, heart swelling with pride.

She spotted him instantly, and with tears brimming, she whispered silently, *"Papa."*

At that moment, nothing else mattered, not the sacrifices, not the years of restraint, not even the ambitions he had quietly buried. That moment was his reward. She was his victory, his proof, his legacy.

Her First Steps Into the Legacy

By now, Samarth's company stood tall—a respected name with a four-floor head office in Delhi and branches across India. What had once been a dim rented room with a flickering tube light was now a landmark of trust.

But the real resurrection was not in bricks, mortar, or trophies. It was in watching Misha step through the same doors he once entered with trembling hands, not as a child seeking her father, but as a young woman carrying his dream forward.

He saw her in meetings—listening intently, taking notes, asking sharp questions. Her voice, though new, carried a conviction that startled seasoned managers. She was bold where he had once been cautious, curious where he had once been doubtful. And as he watched, Samarth felt his heart thrum with something deeper than pride: renewal.

He realised the company was no longer only the repository of his scars and struggles. Its future would carry her fire, her vision. His legacy was no longer solitary—it was shared.

One evening, as the golden light of dusk fell across the boardroom table, Samarth looked at her and thought: This is the true reward. Not the company itself, but the daughter who will give it a new heartbeat.

Stepping Into the Legacy

The celebration of her Master's degree was more than academic—it was a rite of passage. As they left the convocation hall, Samarth placed his hand gently on her shoulder.

"Now begins the real journey," he said. "What you learnt in books, you must now test in the world."

When she returned to India, the office welcomed her with curious eyes. Employees loyal to Samarth wondered if the young graduate could understand the grit behind the glitter. Some doubted. Some hoped. Samarth, however, simply smiled.

"A true leader," he reminded her, "does not live in someone else's shadow. She learns to walk into the light."

She did exactly that. She observed, learnt, stumbled, and rose. She questioned old systems, experimented with new markets, and introduced digital workflows. Some of her early ideas faltered, but each misstep hardened her resolve. And slowly, what had once been "Samarth's company" became "their vision."

For Samarth, watching her grow was resurrection itself: the boy from Ranchi who had once been mocked for failing exams now saw his bloodline carrying forward a dream that had once seemed impossible. For Misha, every decision was not just business—it was an offering to her father's sacrifices, a prayer carved in action.

The Trial by Fire

For months, all seemed steady. Growth was consistent, clients impressed, employees inspired. But as Samarth had learnt, storms arrive uninvited.

A multinational giant entered the market, armed with deep pockets and ruthless strategies. Clients wavered. Contracts slipped. Whispers swirled in the corridors:

"She's too young."

"She doesn't know how the industry works."

"Maybe it's time Samarth sir returned."

Advisors pressed Samarth to retake command. But he refused. He looked at his daughter and said quietly:

"This is your fire. If you are to lead tomorrow, you must burn through today."

At first, fear coiled inside her. Could she protect what her father had built with sweat and scars? But then she remembered his words from London: Learn the art of entrepreneurship. She realised—this was the exam life had set before her.

She rallied her team. Not as an heiress defending inheritance, but as a leader forging her own fire.

- She re-negotiated contracts, anchoring not on price

but on trust and consistency.

- She launched a digital wing that cut costs and widened reach.
- She called old partners herself, her voice carrying both humility and determination: "This company is not changing its values. Only its wings."

Nights turned sleepless, days relentless. There were setbacks, rejections, even tears. But her will grew sharper with each trial.

And slowly, the tide shifted. Clients returned. New doors opened. Employees who once doubted her now whispered with loyalty: "She carries Samarth sir's fire—and her own."

Resurrection

When the storm cleared, the company was stronger than ever. Not rebuilt—reborn.

In the quiet of the office, Samarth embraced his daughter. His eyes, misted with pride, whispered what his voice could barely carry:

"You are no longer my successor, Misha. You are my equal."

For Samarth, that moment was his resurrection. Betrayal, grief, loneliness—they had once broken him. But now, in his daughter's resilience, he saw the proof that nothing had been wasted. His scars had become her armour. His struggles had become her wings.

And as Misha stood tall in the office he had once filled alone, Samarth knew: his legacy was not ending. It was rising—through her.

The Vision Beyond Borders

The crisis had tested her. The victory had defined her. But what came next would elevate her beyond even Samarth's dreams.

Where Samarth had built a strong national presence, she envisioned a global stage.

"Papa," she told him one evening, as they sat overlooking the city skyline, *"your company gave people trust. Now, I want to give it reach. The world is no longer divided by borders; it is connected by ideas. And our idea deserves to travel."*

With his blessing, she began to shape a new era for the company:

- **Global Expansion:** She opened offices in London, Singapore, and Dubai, turning the once-local brand into an international contender.
- **Innovation & Sustainability:** She tied the company's growth to values that mattered to her generation-green technology, ethical trade, and social responsibility.

- **Digital Leadership:** By integrating AI, automation, and cutting-edge analytics, she ensured the company wasn't just keeping up with the times, but setting the trend.

Investors who had once underestimated her now competed to sit across the table from her. Business magazines featured her as a symbol of *"**Next-Gen Leadership**"*. She was not just running a company, she was shaping an empire.

And yet, through all the glitter and global recognition, one thing remained unchanged. Every boardroom presentation, every speech at international forums, every new partnership began with the same acknowledgment:

"This company is the vision of my father, Samarth. I am merely carrying it forward."

For Samarth, watching her address the world was surreal. The shy young girl who once clutched her graduation gown now stood as a leader commanding respect from across continents.

She had not only preserved his legacy, she had amplified it. She had woven his sacrifices into her innovations, his foundation into her skyscraper.

And together, they had built something larger than both of them:

A legacy that would outlive them.

A Scene of Eternity

The night sky over Geneva shimmered with lights from the grand auditorium. Inside, applause echoed like thunder as she stood on stage, accepting the **Global Leadership Award**. Cameras flashed, voices cheered, but for her, the world narrowed to a single figure in the front row.

Samarth.

His once-broad shoulders had curved with age, his hair silvered, but his eyes were as fierce and alive as the day he first dreamed of this company. He sat quietly, his heart racing, watching his daughter command the stage.

She held the award in her hand and paused. For a moment, the confident businesswoman became the same little girl who once whispered *"Papa"* across a convocation hall. With emotion trembling in her voice, she said:

"This honour belongs to the man who taught me to dream and to dare. To my father, who built the foundation on which I stand. Papa, this is yours."

The hall erupted in applause, but Samarth barely heard it. His eyes blurred with tears as she looked directly at him, her gaze steady, her love unspoken yet thunderously clear.

Time seemed to stop. He saw every moment at once-her first steps, her first day at school, her graduation in London, the battles she had fought in boardrooms, and the empire she now led. She was not just his daughter. She was the living proof that his sacrifices had meaning.

The applause swelled, and she bowed her head. Samarth closed his eyes and smiled, a tear tracing down his cheek.

For in that instant, he knew with certainty:

His legacy was not brick and mortar, not profits or power.

His legacy had a heartbeat.

His legacy had a future.

His legacy had a name-**hers.**

And as father and daughter exchanged a look across the hall, the moment became eternal, etched not just in memory, but in history.

As the ovation in Geneva faded into night, Samarth walked back to his hotel room with a quiet he had not felt in years. Pride had roared in the hall; peace whispered here.

He set the award program on the dresser, loosened his tie, and faced the mirror. In the glass he did not see the man the world applauded; he saw the boy who began with nothing and a father who kept walking.

His reflection did not ask for more—it asked him to remember.

That night, he understood: before a legacy travels the world, it must stand honestly before the mirror at home.

As Samarth watched Misha step into her own light, carrying forward the dream he had once nurtured in the shadows of struggle, his heart felt both full and fragile.

Fatherhood had been his greatest role, love his truest legacy. Yet, as the years folded, he realised that beyond the story of a father and daughter lay another narrative—the story of a man who carried scars, turned them into strength, and left behind lessons that outlived him.

Chapter 11

Legacy and Lessons – A Life Lived, A Story Left Behind

The mirror does not lie.

One evening, as Samarth stood before it, the man staring back was not just today's entrepreneur—it was every version of himself stitched together by failure, loss, resilience, and love. In that reflection, he saw not only the weight of his own journey but also the truth he wished to pass on: **scars that shine are the brightest inheritance we leave the world.**

The Mirror of Memory

Later that night, as he adjusted the cuffs of his shirt before a business event, the mirror in front of him seemed to ripple with time. The tie was perfectly straight, the shoes polished, the man in the reflection composed. But when his eyes met his own, the glass did more than show his face—it became a window into every season of his life.

He didn't just see a middle-aged entrepreneur. He saw the frightened boy from Ranchi who had once trembled under his father's stern gaze, the chalk dust still in the air after another failed exam, the sting of shame burning his cheeks. He saw the restless youth on a motorbike in Lucknow, the wind whipping against his face, cinema tickets crumpled in his pocket, and laughter echoing with the thrill of freedom. He saw the ambitious professional in Delhi, briefcase heavy in his hand, sweat on his brow as he sprinted through metro stations, racing against both time and his own self-doubt.

And then, gleaming in the reflection, stood his XUV—the car that once carried him through city streets like a badge of triumph. He remembered the pride of buying it, the sense that he had finally "arrived." Later, during the pandemic, it would be the same vehicle he sold to keep his employees afloat, its absence a reminder that love sometimes demands sacrifice. The mirror seemed to hold both versions at once: the joy of possession, and the dignity of letting go.

Behind him stood shadows of loss. The sound of Ayush's laughter, suddenly silenced, pressed on his heart like an unfinished song. The ledger with missing numbers whispered of the brother who had betrayed him with a shrug. The cold words of his cousin during the pandemic replayed—*make a presentation if you want help*—while his own exhaustion blurred the slides on his laptop screen. And then Dixit, the boss who dangled money like a trap, his smooth voice still curling in Samarth's ears. Each betrayal left a scar, and in the mirror they glowed faintly, not as wounds but as reminders etched into stone.

Yet, in the reflection, light flickered too. He saw Ruhi in the kitchen, cumin sizzling in the pan, her soft humming calming the chaos of his thoughts. He saw the first night he held Misha, her tiny fingers curling around his own, her breath warm against his chest—the moment life gave him a new centre of gravity. He saw his employees gathered in dimly lit rooms during the pandemic, faces lined with worry but eyes shining with loyalty, standing by him even when survival seemed impossible.

And above all, he saw resilience. Every version of himself—child, lover, husband, father, entrepreneur—stood layered within the man now straightening his tie. The boy who fell. The man who rose. Again and again.

The mirror spoke without words: life isn't made of separate chapters that close neatly when the next begins. Life is a single flowing story, every wound echoing into the next triumph, every scar lighting the path for the next lesson. The reflection didn't divide his past and present—it stitched them together.

Samarth exhaled, his hand lingering on the cuff of his shirt. For a moment, the room dissolved—the ticking clock, the polished desk, the event waiting outside. It was just him, his reflection, the faint memory of his motorbike, the pride of his XUV, and the echo of a journey stitched with grief and grace.

And in that reflection, he finally smiled—not with pride, not with vanity, but with peace. Because he knew: every version of himself still lived inside him, and together they had carried him here.

Lessons From the Journey

The reflection stirred memories that rose like lanterns in the dark, each one glowing with its own lesson.

- **Pain is a teacher.** Failing exams did not ruin him—it carved resilience. His father's sternness was not cruelty but chiselling. Ayush's drowning was not just loss, it was the birth of purpose. Pain had been brutal, but it was also the most honest classroom.

- **Love must have boundaries.** He had once given endlessly—money, time, trust—until there was nothing left but exhaustion. He learned, slowly and painfully, that love without respect becomes a wound. Boundaries, he realised, are not walls; they are the guardrails that keep love alive.

- **Success is not wealth.** There were months when his account read zero, and yet he stood tall, because dignity was never bankrupt. Resilience, he discovered, was a currency no bank could measure, and persistence was the real interest earned.

- **Scars are strength.** Each betrayal left its mark—the shrug of a friend who turned into a thief, the silence of family who refused to help, the suffocating grip of power disguised as aid. Every scar hurt. But scars were not shame. They were proof he survived.

- **Legacy is not numbers, but hearts.** His daughter's pride, his wife's quiet faith, his employees' loyalty—these were his monuments. Not marble, not glass towers, but beating hearts that carried his story forward.

Each lesson came wrapped in nights of anguish, but each one left him standing straighter. He realised that life was never about avoiding wounds—it was about learning how to wear them as armour.

Conversations with Himself

At night, when the city outside his terrace pulsed with restless lights, Samarth whispered into the wind. Sometimes it was to Ayush. Sometimes to himself. Sometimes to a God who answered only in silence.

"Have I done enough? Have I carried my duty well? Have I given too much, or too little?"

There was no voice from the sky. But in the hollow of his chest, another voice stirred—the voice of experience. It told him he was not perfect. He had stumbled, cried in hidden corners, broken down in solitude. But he had never betrayed his conscience. And sometimes, that is all a man can ask for: not perfection, but fidelity to his truth.

The terrace became his confessional, his temple, his classroom. And slowly he learned to trust the silence. The silence, he realised, was not empty—it was his own soul answering back.

The Daughter's Eyes

Misha had grown into a woman now, but in her eyes Samarth often saw the child she once was. Wide, curious, and full of awe for a man who felt ordinary but looked like a hero through her gaze.

One evening she said softly, "Papa, you taught me

that life is not about never falling, but about rising every time."

Her words struck him deeper than applause ever had. Because behind those words lay decades—nights when he walked home with empty pockets, mornings when he wore the same old shirt but still smiled, evenings when betrayal bled him dry. He had been broken a thousand times, but he had risen a thousand and one. And she had been watching.

So he began to prepare her—not with sermons, but with conversations. He asked her opinions on world events, listened to her as though she were already shaping nations. He told her stories of contracts lost and betrayals endured. He wanted her to know that leadership is not titles, but scars carried with grace.

"Strength," he told her once, "is not pretending you are unbreakable. Strength is breaking—and still choosing to heal."

She nodded, her eyes glistening, and in that moment he knew: his greatest legacy would not be his company, but his daughter's courage.

The Company as Legacy

The office building in Delhi was four floors tall now, humming with ideas and pride. Branches stood across India. Yet Samarth never saw it as "his company."

He saw it as a family.

- Every book printed was not a product; it was a bridge to a child's tomorrow.
- Every school he worked with was not a client; it was a partner in shaping the nation.
- Every employee was not staff; they were kin who had shared hunger and hope with him.

He remembered the dim rented room where it all began, the flicker of a tube light, the piles of unpaid bills, and Ruhi's hand steadying his trembling fingers. To see it now alive with colour and laughter was like watching ashes bloom into flowers.

And yet, Samarth believed the company was only phase one. "Books were my world," he told Misha, "but the digital sky will be yours.

Together, they began launching EdTech projects—AI-driven classrooms, coding for children, digital literacy in villages.

Awards lined the shelves. National honours, global recognitions, trophies glittered in glass cabinets. But to Samarth, none of these shone brighter than the sparkle in a child's eyes who had learned something new, or the steady smile of an employee whose salary arrived on time even in crises.

That was the true company he had built—trust, not towers.

The Scar That Remains

And yet, amidst the applause, one absence remained. **Ayush.**

Every victory, every contract, every award was silently dedicated to him. Samarth whispered into the void: *This is for you, beta.*

The wound never healed, but it transformed into a compass. Ayush's absence taught him compassion. It reminded him that life is fragile, that love is not measured by time but by memory.

Some nights, he still wept for him. But those tears were not weakness; they were proof that love never dies—it simply changes form, carried forward in choices and legacies.

The Season Summoned (Reprise)

When Samarth looked back, life did not unfold as chapters neatly divided by years. It revealed itself in **seasons**—each one shaping him, scarring him, yet leaving him standing.

There was the season of **Ranchi**, where he first carried the burden of failure. A frightened boy who stumbled in exams, who trembled under his father's stern silence, who wondered if he was meant only to be ordinary. But Ranchi also gave him his first glimpse of grit—the raw truth that failure does not define you, but prepares you.

Then came the season of **Lucknow**, painted with contradictions. It was the city of first pay cheques and reckless bike rides, of cinema-hall kisses and hurried romances. It was also the city that taught him responsibility—the weight of a wife's devotion, the quiet rituals of love stitched into cumin-scented kitchens and ironed shirts. Lucknow was youth colliding with maturity, freedom tempered by devotion. It gave him not only memories, but the foundation of his career.

From there, the season of **Delhi** began—a city of ambition, sweat, and sacrifice. Here, Samarth rose higher than he ever imagined, called back to the head office to shoulder bigger responsibilities. Delhi was where his daughter, Misha, was born—his living anchor, his reason to fight through nights of despair. But Delhi was also a crucible of betrayals, where scars were branded onto his faith.

And then—the darkest season of all—**loss**. The day Ayush drowned, the laughter of childhood was silenced forever. That single moment carved a hollow so deep it never closed. Every contract signed, every cheque cleared, every triumph afterward carried a whispered dedication: *This is for you, beta.* Ayush became both his wound and his vow—the scar that never healed, yet never let him quit.

But the seasons did not relent. Betrayals struck one after another:

- **By man**, when a colleague he called brother siphoned money and dismissed trust as a weakness.
  By nature, when Covid-19 swept across the world, suffocating his company and forcing him to pawn cars and jewellery just to pay his people.
  By blood, when a cousin brother on his maternal side mocked his desperation, asking for presentations instead of offering compassion, and relatives demanded equity like vultures circling his pain.
  By power, when Dixit—once his boss, now an industry giant—offered money but only as chains, a deal designed not to save him but to suffocate his dream.

Each betrayal was a knife. Each scar another reminder that trust, family, power, even fate itself could turn against you.

Yet, there were other seasons too.

The season of **emptiness**, when he walked home with pockets bare but head held high, choosing to pay his employees before himself.

The season of **loneliness**, when he rode his bike into the night, speaking only to the river and to the soul of Ayush.

The season of **fatherhood**, when Misha's small arms around his neck reminded him that even heroes are allowed to cry.

And finally, the season of **breakthroughs**, when contracts returned, salaries flowed, and the company rose from the ashes—not untouched, but unbroken.

Through Ranchi's failures, Lucknow's contradictions, Delhi's betrayals, and the haunting loss of Ayush, Samarth discovered one truth: seasons are not meant to destroy us, but to forge us. *Each wound cut him open, but each scar stitched him stronger.*

When the fog of time cleared, his company still stood—not flawless, but alive.

And so did he.

The seasons had stripped him of illusions, of comfort, of blind trust. But they had left behind something indestructible: **resolve.**

Resolve to rise.

Resolve to endure.

Resolve to turn scars into stories, and stories into lessons.

Samarth emerged not bitter, but forged in fire. Not untouched, but unshaken. His scars, once wounds, had become the signature of survival—the proof that even in betrayal, even in loss, even in emptiness, a man can choose to rise.

A Message to the World

Samarth's life was never about perfection. It was about survival, about falling and rising, about walking through seasons that tore at his skin and still daring to love. And as he stood at the edge of his journey, he knew he did not want to leave behind only buildings, awards, or contracts. He wanted to leave behind a truth for anyone who would listen.

He wanted the world to know that **failure is not final**. A boy once shamed for failing exams in Ranchi could still grow into a man trusted by thousands. Scars of failure are not stains—they are maps, showing you where you must climb again.

He wanted the world to remember that **love is strength, not sacrifice**. In Lucknow, he had learnt that love was not only in fiery romance but in quiet rituals—the ironing of a shirt, the sharing of tea, the hand that waits in silence. True love never diminishes you; it steadies you.

He wanted the world to understand that **loss is a teacher**. Ayush's absence was the scar that never healed, but also the proof that love is stronger than time.

The people we lose never leave us—they live in our choices, in our courage, in the way we rise after falling.

He wanted the world to accept that **betrayal is not the end**. By man, by nature, by blood, and by power—he had been broken. But scars are not signs of defeat. They are the proof that you endured what others could not. Trust carefully, yes. But never stop trusting, for without it, life becomes only survival, never joy.

He wanted the world to believe that **success is not measured in wealth, but in resilience**. His accounts had once been empty, his cars sold, his jewellery pawned, his pride tested. Yet he stood, because resilience is the one currency that never loses value.

And above all, he wanted the world to see that **legacy is not brick and mortar—it is love carried forward**. His empire was not the head office in Delhi or the branches across India. It was Misha's courage, his employees' loyalty, the sparkle in a child's eyes when they held one of his books. That was the real inheritance he left behind.

To anyone who would listen, his message was simple:

- *Cry when **life breaks** you, but rise when the **tears dry**.*
- *Trust, but with boundaries that protect your soul.*
- *Love deeply, but never at the cost of yourself.*

- *Do your duty, but let it be guided by conscience, not greed.*
- *Build something that breathes after you are gone—not just wealth, but wisdom, not just monuments, but memories.*

Scars do not make you weaker. They make you real. They make you shine.

And if his story meant anything at all, it was this:

you may be betrayed, you may lose, you may fall—but you can still rise, and in rising, you become someone the world can never forget.

Epilogue

A Letter From My Heart

My dear reader,

If these words have found you, I invite you to pause. Close your eyes for a breath. Call to mind the faces that matter most—your parents, your children, your siblings, your friends. Now ask yourself, with brutal honesty: *Do they know?* Do they know how much you love them? Do they feel, in the marrow of their bones, how deeply they matter to you?

For if life has chiselled one truth into me, it is this: time is merciless, love is fragile, and relationships are the only true fortune we will ever own.

I began as a boy from Ranchi, laughed at for failing exams, carrying dreams too heavy for my small pockets. I became a young man chasing freedom on a motorbike, scarred more than saved, betrayed more than believed. I endured nights so lonely I whispered into the darkness, *"Why does everyone I trust leave me?"* I stumbled through storms with nothing in my wallet but everything in my heart.

I lost my nephew, Ankush, and with him, a part of my soul. His laughter vanished into silence that still echoes in my nights. And yet, from that silence, I built. Not out of hunger for success, but out of remembrance. I built to keep his joy alive in every corridor, in every book, in every child's smile touched by my work.

What the world called a business, I called love.

A second-hand desk became a sanctuary.

Every book printed was a prayer.

Every child who turned those pages was a promise.

Every employee who grew within my walls was a heartbeat of my own.

And through it all, my daughter Muskaan became my compass. She saw the tears I thought were hidden. She felt the storms I never named. She learnt from my silences as much as from my words. She grew to understand that strength is not the absence of failure, but the decision to rise again and again.

Now, as she steps into the company once carried on my broken shoulders, I feel a pride that no award could ever give me. The dream is no longer mine alone. It belongs to her. To the classrooms she will revolutionise. To the children who will find wings through her courage. To the generations yet unborn who will rise on the foundation of what we built.

And so, my dear reader, let me leave you with the distilled lessons of my journey:

- Cry without shame. Tears are not weakness; they are evidence of love.
- Trust—but always with boundaries. Respect is the true currency of all bonds.
- Do your duty, but never sell your soul. Your conscience must remain your clearest compass.
- Love—not blindly, not endlessly, but wisely. Love that honours, protects, and uplifts.
- Build something that endures. Not merely wealth, but memories, values, and dreams that outlive you.

Because one day, when your titles fade and your wealth scatters, the only treasure left will be love. Love in your child's laughter. Love in your friends' stories. Love in the strangers whose lives you touched without ever knowing.

If my story proves anything, let it be this: scars are not endings. They are beginnings—the ink of wisdom, the armour of resilience, the proof that you lived.

Carry them with dignity. Rise from them with courage. And pass on not just what you earned, but what you learnt.

My story bows here. But my daughter's story begins. And that, perhaps, is the purest victory of all.

With sincerity and fire,

—Santosh Verma